CW00375827

Sophie de Fontenoy, an orphan of the French Revolution, attracts the eye of Napoleon and becomes known as the Emperor's Jewel. He arranges her marriage to his youngest general, Raoul St. Estèphe, whose family destroyed hers in the Revolution and now occupy her family home, the Château d'Argent. Humiliated by the boorish Raoul and his relatives, Sophie dreads the forthcoming marriage. Fate intervenes dramatically when she discovers a handsome English spy, Edmund Apsley, lying wounded in the château grounds. Can she help the fugitive to escape when she is so jealously watched? What future can there be for her love of an enemy of France when Napoleon himself is her protector?

By the same author in Masquerade

LADY OF DARKNESS

The Emperor's Jewel
Lisa Montague

MILLS & BOON LIMITED
London · Sydney · Toronto

First published in Great Britain 1979
by Mills & Boon Limited,
17–19 Foley Street, London W1A 1DR

© Lisa Montague 1979
Australian copyright 1979
Philippine copyright 1979

ISBN 0 263 72883 8

The text of this publication or any part thereof may not be
reproduced or transmitted in any form or by any means, elec-
tronic or mechanical, including photocopying, recording, stor-
age in an information retrieval system, or otherwise, without
the written permission of the publisher.

This book is sold subject to the condition that it shall not, by
way of trade or otherwise, be lent, resold, hired out or otherwise
circulated without the prior consent of the publisher in any form
of binding or cover other than that in which it is published and
without a similar condition including this condition being
imposed on the subsequent purchaser.

Set in 11 on 12½ pt VIP Plantin

Made and printed in Great Britain by
C. Nicholls & Company Ltd.,
The Philips Park Press, Manchester

CHAPTER
ONE

THE pendant was the size of a pigeon's egg – a heart-shaped oval surrounded by a blaze of diamonds, and surmounted with the initial "N" fashioned in more diamonds of the first water. It nestled against the cream satin lining of a leather box decorated with the Emperor's own cipher, where even the dull light could not quench its sparkling iridescence.

"The Emperor's jewel!" Madame St. Estèphe exclaimed rapturously for about the eighth time, her protruding brown eyes fastened on the bauble as if it were the talisman to all the power and glory the world could offer.

Her daughter, Madame Marie le Corde, gazed at it hungrily, like someone who has been deprived of nourishment for many days.

"Vulgar! That's what I'd call it," muttered old Léontine, just out of earshot, pretending to be busy sorting through Sophie's silk stockings, but really in order not to leave her alone with those two harpies. In her opinion, Mademoiselle Sophie ought to feel insulted rather than honoured that the upstart little Corsican, who had the audacity to have himself crowned Emperor of France, should present her with such a monstrosity. She gave Vit, Sophie's great wolfhound, a prod with her foot. The dog opened a baleful eye, glanced towards the goddess he had known since his puppy days to make sure all was well with her, and then resumed his nap.

At least half an hour had passed since a lackey in the imperial colours had delivered this gift to the Château d'Argent, but Sophie's delicate fingers still hovered uncertainly above the costly trinket. Her cheeks wore a deep flush that owed nothing to the rouge pot while she re-read the Emperor's accompanying note, which had first been ecstatically perused by Madame St. Estèphe, then by Madame le Corde, and lastly by the lady to whom it was written:

Mademoiselle de Fontenoy, may I offer you this paltry token with my congratulations on the occasion of your formal betrothal to General Raoul St. Estèphe. I take great pleasure in being instrumental in uniting you, a veritable jewel of the old French nobility, with the lifeblood of the new France. Through this commingling of your blood may all the old enmity between aristocracy and revolutionary be erased so that your many children will know nothing but harmony and prosperity. Tomorrow, the Empress and I shall do our utmost to attend your betrothal celebrations, where I hope to feast my eyes on the Emperor's Jewel.

It was not because the St. Estèphes had once been peasantry that Sophie hated them with every fibre of her being, believing death preferable to exchanging marriage vows with Raoul. After all, the greater proportion of her eighteen years had been spent among the humblest of fisherfolk. By marrying him she would be betraying her beloved parents. For it was his family who had caused the de Fontenoys to be butchered during the Reign of Terror.

Then, under the new order, the St. Estèphes had seized possession of much de Fontenoy wealth. Now, it was Madame St. Estèphe who was decked out each day with jewels Sophie could just remember around her

Mamma's lovely neck, particularly the famous pearls brought back from the east by an early de Fontenoy ancestor. How ironic to return finally to the Château d'Argent, where she had been born and spent her first years, as an unwilling bride at the command of the Emperor, who regarded this marriage as an excellent way of restoring to Mademoiselle de Fontenoy the rights and wealth long since lost.

After the wedding, she would continue to reside at this château or at the great mansion in Paris, formerly the de Fontenoy Hôtel, for Madame St. Estèphe had declared it most unsuitable for a young bride to live alone, once Raoul had returned to his regiment. "Besides," she had said with an insinuating smile that displayed blackened teeth, "you will probably be in too interesting a condition to run a household. Although there will be no time for a honeymoon because of this wretched war with England, I cannot believe my Raoul will leave you without hope of a babe. The St. Estèphes are well known for their full quivers."

Whenever Sophie's mind dragged her thoughts unhappily to the issue of marriage, her cheeks flamed with anger and shame. Ah yes, she did love babies. All the fisherwomen used to bring her their newborn to soothe with her gentle hands and pretty voice, while they gutted the fish the menfolk had just caught. As Sophie cuddled and sang to those morsels of flesh, her girlish daydreams had naturally centred on the babies that might one day be hers . . . and of their father, a man she could love and honour . . . a man with all the attributes of some knight from the ancient tales of chivalry . . . a man quite unlike the crude-tongued Raoul St. Estèphe.

Sophie had never hankered after riches, comfort or

position, for these had been snatched from her before they could acquire any meaning. Only through the fierce love and protection of her wet-nurse, Léontine, had she escaped her parents' fate. Despite her own peasant origin, Léontine was a devout monarchist who believed in the old social order, and she had sworn to the Comtesse de Fontenoy to protect the little one with her life.

In the dawn of the same morning that the rabble had broken into the château, Léontine had slipped away, carrying a sleepy child, followed by the puppy Vit – the runt of the litter recently born to the Comte's favourite bitch. Its devotion to the little mademoiselle had exceeded its strength so that soon it, too, had to be borne in the nurse's strong arms.

Léontine had taken the girl and the pup to a remote village in Brittany where her own people lived. Citizeness Sophie was safe among the great brood of children. There had been no lessons in dancing, deportment, music, poetry or flirtation – the schoolroom diet of a young female aristocrat – but instead she had learned to spin, to sew, to cook, to tend a vegetable patch, and even to gut fish and sail a boat. Only Sophie's dainty hands and feet and her fragility hinted that she had not been born to this rustic existence. Not that anyone minded that. Indeed, all had worshipped the golden-haired nymph with the happy knack of delighting people. When she grew towards womanhood more than one fisherlad cast a longing eye at her, dreaming of love.

Yet none had stolen so much as a kiss. Vit had grown into too big a brute to permit that. The only person with whom he was as gentle as a mouse was Sophie. To Léontine he demonstrated a rough but amiable camaraderie; they were after all devoted to the same cause. She, too, fended off the would-be lovers, for she believed her vow to the Comtesse included returning her daughter to a more fitting society. To allow the girl to form an attachment with one of Léontine's own young relatives – however sober and industrious – would be to break faith with the dead.

Once a degree of stability obtained under the new Consulate, and the surviving aristocrats had begun drifting back to France, Léontine had conducted an unwilling Sophie to Paris to the Lamberts, who were distant cousins to the de Fontenoys, but to Sophie they were complete strangers. The girl saw no reason why she could not remain for ever with the fisherfolk who were all the family and friends she possessed. She found the Lamberts' elegant house and manners artificial and stifling, and for the first time learned that smiling lips could lie.

Opportunists as shrewd as the Lamberts, who had grown rich from dealing in armaments, could not fail to recognise the potential of their young relative's unusual beauty. It could well lead its owner, and consequently her relatives, to greater things, particularly in the medley of backgrounds which had begun to meld into a new aristocracy around the First Consul, Napoleon Bonaparte.

Sophie was commanded to forget her old skills and hoydenish ways, and was instructed in dancing, singing, deportment, and a smattering of all those improving subjects which, like jewels, enhanced a fashionable young lady.

Sophie was also urged to forget her past companions. Instead Madame Lambert found her new, exciting company. She introduced her cousin to the First Consul's wife, the almost legendary Josephine, who was so enraptured by Mademoiselle de Fontenoy that the girl became a regular visitor to the Tuileries. Amongst the painted, sophisticated ladies, volubly discussing their amours and divorces, Sophie's unspoilt charm was a breath of air in early spring – a reminder of youth, virtue, dreams and romance.

She was much admired by the gentlemen, not the least of whom to be captivated was the First Consul himself. Tongues wagged mightily, eyes searched for a delicious scandal, and Josephine's smile became a trifle strained as she watched her husband dance with the girl possessed of such childlike radiance. Yet it was Sophie's unworldliness that guarded her where a more knowing beauty might have seen the heady advantage of entangling the man bent on turning republic into empire.

Her future was to be guided by him, the Emperor had declared passionately at the ball following his coronation, so that the glittering throng stared with amused curiosity at the blushing girl whose golden curls outshone even Josephine's diadem. She was the Emperor's own jewel, to be bestowed on the most worthy of his new subjects. As a military man, Napoleon not unnaturally selected for this reward his youngest general, Raoul St. Estèphe.

Fate had come full circle to mock her. A de Fontenoy had missed death at the hands of the St. Estèphes only to be returned to them in marriage. In Sophie's eyes this was their final triumph over her dead parents, but the Lamberts were shocked that her innocent mind could harbour such dangerous thoughts and bade her keep them locked in her heart. All *their* fondest hopes had been realised. Through Sophie's connections they were invited to court, and certainly they made no objection when it was suggested she live at the Château d'Argent near the Somme estuary, so the young couple might spend what little time Raoul could steal from his military duties at Boulogne in getting to know each other. In the current climate of war, most couples were lucky if they had ten days to get acquainted, let alone a formal betrothal. For Sophie, half an hour was quite sufficient to know she hated Raoul and his family.

The St. Estèphes magnanimously disregarded Sophie's lack of fortune, for by accepting the Emperor's jewel they were gaining further favour and attention. While Napoleon doted on the girl their star was in the ascendant, and both Madame and Monsieur St. Estèphe talked long into the night about what honours would be conferred on her children, their grandchildren. They neither remembered nor cared about the part they had played in making this daughter-to-be an orphan.

Even the small circular boudoir Sophie had been given as her own was a poignant reminder of the past. It had been her nursery, and she had never quite forgotten the view from its windows. Now the leaded casements showed the summer storm had turned the noon sky evening dark. Raindrops drummed diagonally against the panes like regiments of soldiers marching on manoeuvres. Clouds of rain scudded across the parkland, blotting out the ornamental lake, the rotunda, the bright formal flower beds and the full greenery of high summer.

It seemed to Sophie that all heaven wept in unison with her heart. Not that her small oval face revealed this inner anguish. That would have given her vindictive sister-in-law-to-be too much pleasure. Besides, what good was weeping? There was no escape from this destiny any more than her dearest Mamma and Papa had managed to cheat Madame Guillotine. She was doomed to marry Raoul, whatever either felt about the other, for neither of them dared flout the Emperor's wishes.

True, General St. Estèphe made no pretence at caring for that "virginal little doll", as he slightingly dubbed her to his friends and family. He would rather have taken a more dashing creature with plenty of land and tin of her own, but what did preference matter when the Emperor had promised him a Marshal's baton as a wedding gift? That was worth marrying the devil's daughter for, let alone this tiny sprig of aristocracy.

Only Léontine recognised that her young lady's great grey eyes were shadowed with grief, understanding the reason, but then she had known Sophie since birth, had nursed her at her own breast giving her the milk meant for the baby that had died in its first hours, and had witnessed the wondrous transformation of a long-legged fragile child into beauteous womanhood.

She blamed herself for Sophie's plight, and would have sold her own soul if she could have rescued her from it. Léontine was even forced to recognise that it would have been preferable for Mademoiselle de Fontenoy to have married a decent fisherboy rather than this coarse military sensualist. All she could hope to do was to stay close beside her little lady and defend her from the worst.

"You were born under a fortunate star, my precious Sophie," Madame St. Estèphe said ponderously. She set great store by how the movements of the celestial bodies affected those of mortals on earth. Had not the almanac in the year of Raoul's birth predicted great things for those born at that hour in the house of Scorpio? Now, he was one of Napoleon's most valued generals, and as soon as this marriage with Sophie de Fontenoy was solemnised he would become the youngest-yet Marshal of France. Indeed, the stars had not lied about her son's future.

For the fifth time she rearranged her overlarge lace cap, peering into the dressing-mirror to admire the effect. Although she and Marie had come to the boudoir to advise how Sophie's hair should be dressed for tomorrow's ball, so far they had spent the hour preening themselves and discussing their own ball gowns.

"I doubt our sweet Sophie understands just how lucky she is, Mamma, or how valuable is that trinket the Emperor sent her. Remember, she has spent her days with people who dig in the mud for worms!" Marie's small laugh was malicious, and the little teeth pressing against too-red lips were somewhat reminiscent of a rodent's. "Look at her face. Who would think it belonged to a maiden on the eve of her betrothal ball? Heaven knows, Martin and I had no such enjoyable preliminaries on our marriage! Raoul brought him home. He asked Papa for my hand. Two weeks later we were married."

And, have fought like the proverbial cat and dog ever since, amended Sophie silently. Martin Le Corde was quite a pleasant fellow, even if he were Raoul's best friend, but with Marie as a wife it was little wonder he had taken to drink and gambling as the panacea to those everlasting quarrels.

Madame Le Corde examined Sophie's lovely but unsmiling features with critical eyes, and then turned back to her own reflection. It had taken her new maid a good hour that morning to prepare her face, applying the gold paint specially created for the Empress Josephine to the eyelids, so it did not seem at all just that Sophie, who wore no more than an unfashionable whisper of rouge, should look so much better. Like the Empress and her entourage, Marie spent a small fortune on cosmetics with Martin the Parisian perfumier. Like the Empress's, Marie's thick make-up had begun to crack in the heat, showering her shoulders and bodice with a fine white dust.

Impatiently she brushed at this powder, and smoothed the embroidered, heavy silk robe with hands so beringed and braceleted it was difficult to see the supporting flesh. The gown had been created by Leroy, Josephine's own designer, and must therefore be the last word in fashion. It was certainly very expensive at two thousand francs, more than many a lady spent on her court dress; and Martin had remarked acidly that Napoleon might empty the coffers of Europe to clothe his wife, but he, Martin, had only his army pay to dress Marie. Like all her husband's other remonstrations, this one had fallen on deaf ears.

Yet, the bright peacock silk did not suit Marie's sallowness. Her dark brows creased slightly. The frown emphasised a permanently disagreeable expression. She was one of those unfortunate creatures, born never to be content. Now, she was wondering how it could be possible that Sophie should look so stylish and dainty in a simple grey chiffon trimmed only with rose satin ribbons that any serving-wench might disdain to wear.

"You would think," Marie continued her goading relentlessly, "that a girl who had the wonderful chance to play a part at the coronation would look more cheerful, especially as she is shortly to be enfolded in the warm embraces of my dear brother."

Sophie lowered her eyes. It was not modesty, but shame: that she, the sole survivor of one of France's ancient families, should have been among the twelve virgins of the old aristocracy chosen to carry candles and escort His Holiness, the Pope, at the crowning of the Corsican who had risen to power over so many noble corpses.

As for Raoul's embraces, her soul shuddered with repugnance. This was not maidenly embarrassment, for growing up in the small fishing community Sophie could scarce avoid witnessing the most fundamental facts of life and death. This knowledge of passion and birth did not affront her in the least, only the anticipation of sharing them with a man for whom she felt no affection, who obviously did not care for her.

Oh, Raoul was good enough looking with his dark hair and florid complexion. Many a girl might even consider the young General handsome, but beneath heavy black brows that met above the bridge of his nose, the large dark eyes were set too close, giving him a sly appearance as if even at his most good-humoured he was sneering at others. Had his name not been St. Estèphe, Sophie doubted she would have trusted him. Despite her elegant new life, she still judged people and situations in the down-to-earth terms of her old, humble one. She guessed the fisherfolk would not have bought a horse from such as Raoul lest it be stolen or quite other than described by his glib tongue.

As yet, no man had kissed her lips, but Sophie had tried to imagine what it must be like to exchange ardent caresses. Somewhere, her dream insisted, was the man in whose arms she could be safe and happy, whose kisses would send fire racing through her veins, making her heedless of all save love. Raoul was not that person, and now she knew she would never meet such a man. Her future was signed and sealed and belonged irrevocably to the St. Estèphes.

"You are right, Marie. Do try to look more cheerful, Sophie. Anyone would think your future husband was an eighty-year-old dotard, to judge by your long face, and not my charming boy," Madame St. Estèphe said reproachfully, and then returned to the topic that had occupied almost every waking minute of the past five days – the lavish preparations for the betrothal ball. "Merely consider all we are spending on these celebrations, even sending to Paris so that everything may be of the best and most fashionable, although we are almost in the middle of nowhere."

"Ices specially ordered from Frascati, and the choicest candelabra and epergnes from Odiot, since the château does not possess enough to make a splendid show." Animation shone through the heavy gauze of powder to mottle the plump cheeks bright red. "The Emperor is no trencherman. I hear he spends less than fifteen minutes at dinner, and once sent back as many as twenty-two chickens at the Tuileries because none pleased his palate. But I guarantee that will not happen here. We shall tempt him with such succulent dishes that it will be long before he forgets the St. Estèphe feast.

"We have truffled turkeys, Toulouse pasties, the red-legged partridges from Perigord stuffed with pâté de foie . . . and as for those Pithiviers larks," she smacked her lips as if already savouring the toothsome song birds that the cook would bone and bake in pastry cases. "What a pike we have for those who favour fish! I declare not even the Emperor has been served with a bigger one. The fisherman who caught it swore to me *he* had never before seen a fish of such magnitude in the Somme."

Here Sophie suppressed a smile, and saw in the looking-glass that Léontine was grinning wickedly to herself. They both knew full well how any fisherman wanting the highest price from those with too much money and great pretensions always vowed the fish in question was a unique monster of its species!

"And as for the centre-piece," Madame St. Estèphe drew such a deep proud breath that her capacious bosom threatened to overflow from the bodice of her Grecian gown, "ah, that is really something. A true work of art. The huge cake, in nougat, sponge, and spun sugar, represents Napoleon's great victory at Lodi in '96. I am certain he will take this as a subtle compliment to his military prowess –" she giggled excitedly. "The major-domo is instructed to serve him his favourite Chambertin. For the rest of us there will be more than enough champagne to bathe in. Now, Sophie, doesn't that warrant a more carefree expression on a fiancée's face?"

"I did not ask for any of these things, madame," Sophie reminded her, and with gentle irony added, "Indeed, I judge them quite superfluous in this instance."

Madame St. Estèphe looked as shocked as if her daughter-to-be had uttered a profanity in public. "What an odd child you are! We cannot permit the betrothal of our only son, a future Marshal of France, to go unmarked by great festivity because his bride once lived like a fishwife." She changed the subject abruptly.

"Something must be done with all that hair," Madame St. Estèphe announced tragically, looking at

Sophie's unbound tresses as if they were so many hanks of rope rather than a waist-length cape of corn-coloured silk. "Shall my maid dress it for you tomorrow so that at least it has a semblance of fashion?"

"Oh no, Léontine will arrange my hair. She is the only one who can manage it."

"Which explains why it is always in the rearguard of fashion," Marie said acidly.

It was Léontine who interposed triumphantly, "But the Emperor has frequently complimented Mademoiselle Sophie on the abundance and sheen of her hair."

"That is beyond understanding," Madame St. Estèphe sniffed. "He positively discourages ladies appearing at court anything but heavily painted and professionally coiffured. Why, when one poor creature forgot her rouge he was cruel enough to say she looked like a corpse and ordered her to paint her face at once. Yet, as far as Sophie is concerned, our Emperor has a blind spot. She can be totally unpainted, with her hair anyhow, like some peasant girl, and he pronounces that beautiful."

What she failed to recognise was that for Napoleon, Sophie's natural loveliness was a bouquet of sweet meadow flowers brought into a stuffy gilt and ormolu drawing-room.

Mother and daughter began trying to arrange Sophie's "impossible" hair that somehow defeated all their efforts, until its owner felt like a poor doll in the clutches of two quarrelsome children. At last, she was forced to protest.

"Ladies, please leave off. My head quite aches."

Regretfully, Madame St. Estèphe set down the brush and pins. "Anyway, once you are married, Raoul will not permit you to keep all that hair," she said darkly, "And we shall have to find you a proper maid. Léontine is too old and stupid to attend to the needs of a Marshal's wife."

Léontine's mouth pressed itself into a bitter line as she thought, without me as an ally they will break her spirit.

Chill fingers clutched at Sophie's heart. For the first time, she realised that marriage would make her the St. Estèphes' prisoner to do with as they liked so long as the Emperor was allowed to see her as he chose. Sophie averted her gaze from Léontine's hurt and angry features in case she gave way to tears and said in level tones, "When the rain stops I must take poor Vit for a walk in the park. The fresh air will clear my head."

Once outside, Sophie thought, I will at least be free from their prying eyes.

At the mention of his name Vit's tail had begun to thump.

"And just how long do you suppose my brother will stand for that great brute?" Marie demanding, casting a look of extreme loathing at the dog. Here was one thing she did not envy, and when Vit lay across the threshold of Sophie's chamber, even she did not presume to enter.

"Vit has always been with me," Sophie tried to keep the catch out of her voice.

"But you must have a dog more suited to a lady of fashion," argued Madame St. Estèphe. She eyed Vit with hostility born of fear. "Something sweet and fluffy to sit on your lap. You can't expect Raoul to allow this beast to cavort about your bedchamber."

"I doubt even the General could stop Vit once he's set his mind on something," Léontine interrupted grimly,

praying the animal would carry off young St. Estèphe
and lose him, and so prevent this whole hideous business. If only she had never taken her little lady to Paris,
but there was no profit in self-recriminations.

"What can General St. Estèphe have against Vit?"
Sophie asked. "The dog only lives to protect me."

Madame St. Estèphe's laughter was forced. She
knew Raoul would not tolerate the dog, and said
brightly: "Ah well, I suppose you two lovebirds will
sort that out when you are wed. A bride can twist her
husband around her little finger."

"Only for the first few days," Marie observed sulk-
ily, "and then all those promises of everlasting devotion grow as sour as milk left in the sun." She looked at
the jewelled watch, hanging from a chain at her neck,
and said, "Raoul and Martin will soon be here." Peering at Sophie, she added gleefully, "It must make you
happy to know your lover is almost at your side."

Marie had divined how much Sophie detested Raoul
and so took joy in alluding to him whenever possible.
Clearly she relished the prospect of another couple
failing to know the happiness that had eluded her!

Defiantly, Sophie smiled. Léontine's heart almost
broke, for she had never seen her angel wear so hard an
expression. "And, no doubt, *you* will be pleased to greet
your husband."

Marie le Corde only scowled in reply. She and Martin
had last parted on less than friendly terms.

Despite the heavy August heat, Sophie felt dreadfully cold, and drew the cashmere shawl close about her
shoulders. One by one the few items dear to her would
be wrested away – Léontine . . . Vit . . . even her hair.
At last, she picked up the Emperor's gift, and held it in
her hand as if weighing it. How cold, heavy and lifeless

it felt. Certainly this was no compensation for what she must lose.

Surely, she thought desperately, there can be no other person in the whole of France caught in such an invidious snare.

But Sophie was wrong.

Only a few miles away a drama was to be enacted that would entrap a stranger – a stranger whose line of fate was destined to cross hers.

CHAPTER
TWO

THE tiny village of Le Crotoy could boast but one estaminet, a humble place known as "The Red Horse". Its gloomy interior smelt strongly of fish and the rough red wine stored in barrels that took up most of the floor space. The customers were mainly fishermen. Few strangers ever passed that way, and those that did could scarcely be dignified by the description of "gentleman", so imagine the landlord's surprise when not one but four gentlemen patronised his café in the same afternoon.

Three of them sat together, two of them officers whose gleaming spurs and buttons brought a touch of drama into the cramped and dusty café. Their companion was older and quieter. His dark hair was streaked with white, and the hollow cheeks suggested both suffering and secrecy. They lounged on high-backed deal settles and the two young men negligently rested their legs across the trestle table. That a quantity of wine had been imbibed was supported by their flushed cheeks, raucous laughter and loud talk.

The fourth man sat alone, concealed from the others by the high back of a settle. His heavily caped coat was dusty, fit only for travelling, but the landlord was in no doubt he, too, must be a gentleman – perhaps an impoverished member of the old aristocracy. The long-fingered hands and sharp-etched profile beneath a profusion of curling blond hair spoke of gentle blood.

The gentleman sat quite still, toying with the beaker of wine before him, contemplating the shadows. Now and then, he would smile as if the smoky obscurity contained delightful images.

Going home to a young wife, or a sweetheart, I'll be bound, concluded the landlord. He had already ascertained the man was no local, for his French had quite another accent. The owner of the Red Horse, who had never been ten miles further than Le Crotoy, presumed he must hail from Lyons or the Auvergne. Anyway, the stranger was quiet and undemanding enough for the landlord to concentrate his attention and ears on the other three, whose demands for wine were growing more frequent and vociferous, and whose conversation had taken a distinctly ribald turn.

He would have been amazed and alarmed to know that the unassuming gentleman was certainly not from that region but an Englishman! A secret agent hurrying back from keeping watch on the troop placements at Boulogne, looking for some fisherman to take him across the Channel when the tide was right. He had momentous news to deliver to his masters: the Corsican, who called himself Emperor of France, had finally decided to give up the intention of invading England, and was to march his army into Austria. It was imperative the British government learn of this as soon as possible so that they could redeploy troops and ships.

The Englishman's name was Edmund Apsley. He was twenty-five years old, and felt very tired. It seemed to him he had been too long away from the green and pleasant England he loved. The last time he had been there was for Serena's wedding. How happy it had made him that his beautiful, accomplished and wilful sister had married his closest friend, Ralph Sherwood. What a wedding it had been, for not only were they celebrating love and hope but also the entire routing of a French spy ring on the Kentish coast, which he, Ralph, and Serena had played no little part in destroying. But, that was quite another story . . .*

How long ago it all seemed. Now, Serena and Ralph were settled quietly on their Patchley estate in Sussex. Not all that quietly, to be sure, for she had but recently been delivered of fine twins – a boy and a girl – whose reputation as lusty screamers had already been relayed to their uncle in France.

The Sherwoods had managed to get their happy news to Edmund through the usual unauthorized route via the smugglers and fishermen on both sides of the Channel who ferried information and passengers for a substantial purse with no questions asked.

So I am an uncle, he thought gaily, his lips curving fondly, although I have yet to see these mites, one of whom has the doubtful privilege of bearing my name. His smile faded, and the clear blue eyes darkened as if their owner's thoughts had grown sombre.

Children, he mused, and the soft warm arms of a loving wife to welcome me to my own hearth – ah, those are things for a man to strive for. Yet, while I lead this kind of precarious existence, what right have I to offer a tender female my name?

Edmund could not imagine any woman loving him the way he would wish. He was scarcely worth it. Since most of his manhood had been devoted to adventure, apart from a little gaming of which he was inordinately fond, Edmund had had little occasion to discover his effect on the fairer sex. He would have been astonished

*See Lady of Darkness.

that many a girl found him devastatingly handsome, casting long-lashed, hopeful glances in his direction, only to discover him too retiring to respond. Anyway, he had long since recognised that he was scarcely likely to find a sweetheart on one of these clandestine expeditions, as he rarely spent enough time in any one place to develop even the beginnings of a friendship.

With some amusement, he guessed that Serena had already set her hand at match-making on his behalf. Now she was so happily wed, his sister could not imagine how anyone on earth could survive without the joyous bonds of matrimony. If he spent long enough at Patchley it would not be for want of her trying that he lacked a wife.

Probably because his mind dwelt on marriage, Edmund began to pay attention to the raucous conversation of the three men at the other table. He could not see them, but their rather slurred voices were too loud to ignore. What he heard made him shake his head ruefully. The poor maiden whose future bridegroom chose to malign her to his cronies while all were clearly in their cups!

"My dear Uncle François," the ungallant fellow was saying. "My little fiancée makes no pretence of caring for me, even to please the Emperor, so I do not expect a very warm welcome in her arms." He laughed. "Anyhow, once we are married that won't matter. There are plenty of beauties yearning to take a gallant officer's mind off his boring matrimonial duties. I confess, here and now to the two of you, that were it not for the Emperor's influence in this business, and his munificent promise, I'd not have taken that virginal little doll as a wife. Oh, I grant you, she is well enough looking. No man would push her from his bed, but all the same –"

Edmund's straight fair eyebrows drew together in disgust. This was the sort of loose talk that any gentleman worth his salt must counter with a challenge. That young military pup should be taught a lesson with the point of a sword, and he hoped the lady had a brother or cousin who would act as teacher! He, of all folk, was hardly in a position to take up the cudgels on behalf of the unknown bride.

"Oh come, Raoul," another voice protested, and Edmund detected a trace of embarrassment there, "Mademoiselle de Fontenoy is an exquisite creature, with the most delightful manners."

"You'd expect *that* from an aristocratic chit," came the bridegroom's churlish response. "Even if she has been brought up among the stench of fish. I daresay she is a beauty – a little too cold-blooded and small-bosomed for my taste. One thing I do not doubt is that her nature is more pleasant than my sister's, eh, old man? Uncle François, here we have a typical example of a hen-pecked husband. What poor Martin suffers from the tantrums of your little niece, Marie, is beyond belief."

His crow of laughter was derisive, as if he found his brother's-in-law predicament vastly entertaining.

The third man spoke with an amused detachment: "Raoul, even though you are a general, you are quite incorrigible to talk so of your own sister, and humiliate poor Captain le Corde. I warrant they shift as well as any other married couple. As you will, too, with your own wife. Besides, look what you gain from wedding the Emperor's favourite! You should count Mademoiselle de Fontenoy's pretty face and ancient lineage an unexpected bonus to a Marshal's baton. When you are a Marshal of France, our family's name will shine with a more deserved lustre than did those of the accursed aristocrats before the Revolution."

Edmund was not so much listening to the gist of this speech as to the speaker's clipped tones. Surely, he knew that voice. He bit at his lower lip, trying to recall where he had heard it. In Boulogne? No. It was further back in time than that. He retraced his movements in Northern France over the past months, but still could not place the voice.

The puzzle irritated him, but this was scarcely the right time to try to solve it. It struck Edmund forcibly that ill-chance had brought an English agent to drink at the same establishment as two French officers – one shortly to become a Marshal! Still, he judged the three too intoxicated to pay him any proper attention. Even if they were ignorant of his presence, caution fostered by experience compelled him to sit without stirring and he hoped they would soon depart. Certainly, it sounded as if they were expected somewhere – perhaps at the unfortunate bride's residence.

Edmund could have wished the bridegroom was a less laggard lover, for he showed no desire to be on his way, particularly while there was wine left to drink. If they stayed tippling much longer, he would miss his chance of finding a boat in time to catch the late afternoon tide. That would mean another night in France . . . another night in jeopardy of being unmasked . . . and another night of delay in imparting valuable information.

The conversation drifted from marriage through lechery to the war, but here the men became more intense and showed their real interest. It was obvious to Edmund that the owner of that familiar voice was well informed about military matters, and even the brag-

gart of a nephew deferred to his uncle's views on warfare.

He must be of some influence, thought Edmund, and
his professional instincts made him curious about just
who the man could be.

"How much longer are we to cool our heels at
Boulogne?" The young General was clearly angry.
"The men are bored and restless. I have even told the
Emperor as much. If we did invade now they would not
fight their best. Too much time has been spent lolling
about in taverns and the arms of women of doubtful
virtue. The Boulogne innkeepers and the wenches must
have made a small fortune from the *Grande Armée*.
They might as well be in league with the accursed
English for they way they are dissipating the men's
energies!"

"I believe the Emperor is currently considering a
fresh scheme," the man called "Uncle François" said
cautiously. "Although what it can be no one is yet
sure."

Edmund smiled grimly to himself. Evidently, he
possessed facts not yet known even to high-ranking
French officers. Therefore the sooner they reached the
British government the more useful would the information prove. Plans might be laid well in advance of
Napoleon's next move – an advantage no nation at war
could afford to overlook.

He could not decide whether this brief halt at Le
Crotoy boded good or ill for his mission, for the village
was situated on the estuary almost opposite Saint
Valéry-sur-Somme – the very town from whence the
last successful invasion of England had begun. It was
there that William, Duke of Normandy, to be known to
the future as "the Conqueror", had amassed his troops.

May Heaven and the stalwart British yeoman, Edmund prayed silently, defend us against any similar mass crossing of the Channel. At least, the uncertain moods of that small stretch of sea have postponed such an invasion. Even the man who seeks to rule the whole of Europe cannot command the waves between our two countries.

This far west of Boulogne the Channel was wider and so took longer to cross, but it was expressly for that reason Edmund had come there. East of Boulogne, where the crossing was narrowest and therefore swift, the coast was vigilantly guarded to prevent just such clandestine passages. So the smugglers and fishermen had taken to plying their nefarious ferry service to and from England around the Somme estuary. Indeed, so sure was Edmund that Le Crotoy and its environs were free of military patrols, that he had been much disturbed to find soldiers at the Red Horse, and only began to feel relieved on hearing the reasons were purely social and not official.

Their last jug of wine had evidently been emptied more speedily than the landlord could have anticipated, for he was not immediately available when the general bawled, "Ho there, fellow! Bring us more of that foul liquid you have the impudence to call wine! Curse the mangy cur! Where has he got to?"

"Be patient, Raoul," urged his brother-in-law. "Probably he went to the cellar to fetch up more wine . . ."

But, the other man ignored this, swore, and rose unsteadily to his feet. Bellowing for the landlord, he stumbled around the settle towards Edmund's corner. By the startled expression on his flushed face, the general had not realised that any stranger had been privy to his conversation. He stared at Edmund as if trying to focus properly. At last, he said roughly,

"Monsieur, we had no idea you were sitting there. We were talking privately. You should have made yourself known to us. I demand an apology. I detest eavesdroppers."

Whereas I, thought Edmund guardedly, make full use of them. His temper was the kind that comes swiftly to the boil, but his training had taught him to curb it. Instead of retorting as his impulses dictated he allowed his brain to take control, and merely shrugged and feigned an embarrassed little smile. "Certainly, I ask your pardon, sir. I am rather tired, and was sitting here dozing over my wine, hardly aware of any company."

The officer surveyed him sullenly, evidently aware he had not displayed himself in the best of lights.

Edmund thought coolly, here is the type who in his cups likes to pick a fight, and while I would relish giving him a sound thrashing I must remember he is not alone and I have too much at stake to risk a brawl.

The General helped himself liberally to Edmund's wine without asking permission. He gulped several mouthfuls, then spat some on the floor. "You're a stranger, aren't you?" he asked curiously, fixing his large dark eyes on the seated man.

Edmund nodded calmly. He had a cover story prepared against all eventualities which explained his accent and reasons for travel. "I am from Bordeaux," he replied. "I work as a clerk in a vintner's office." In his pockets were several fictitious orders for wine, and papers identifying him as Gerard Dupont of Bordeaux.

"Ah, claret country," returned the other affably. "I trust you get to sample the wine sometimes, and do not only have transaction with it on paper. That would be a poor employment."

Edmund grinned, and the conversation might well have ended there, had not the others become inquisitive as to their companion's conversation.

Captain le Corde glanced quickly from his brother-in-law to the stranger, relieved that no argument had developed. "When the landlord replenishes our jug, monsieur," he said courteously, "you must take a glass with us. We are toasting General Raoul St. Estèphe's betrothal. My I introduce myself?"

A drink cannot do any harm, Edmund considered swiftly, as they exchanged names and pleasantries, besides they are only likely to grow suspicious if I refuse and attempt to hurry away. He was about to assent politely when the third man joined them. He walked slowly and painfully, leaning on a stick, as if rheumatics afflicted his joints.

Edmund's features became as still and hard as carved granite. He recognised the newcomer too well and now knew where he had last heard that voice. In England. Then, the man was known as Francis Stephens – the anglicised version of François St. Estèphe. It was he who had headed the spy ring that Edmund, Ralph Sherwood, and Serena had combined to smash.

When the conspirators were rounded up, Stephens had been taken to London, tried, and condemned to death. News had reached Edmund that while awaiting execution the Frenchman had contrived to escape, by bribing a warder. Nobody knew where the fox had gone to earth, but all had assumed he must have returned to his own country. No doubt, those stiff limbs were the heritage of his sojourn in a damp English gaol. Fate had certainly played Edmund false by allowing him to stumble upon the one man in France capable of destroying him.

François St. Estèphe's narrow dark eyes showed he recognised the fair-haired young man, but it was a second or so before the true realisation registered in his brain. The silence seemed like a lifetime of held breath. Raoul stared uncertainly from his uncle to the insignificant wine clerk, aware that here was some association.

Then . . .

"The accursed Englishman," screamed François St. Estèphe, "Apsley! I have him at last. Take him!"

It was Edmund who moved first. He forgot his fatigue. All that mattered was survival and escape. With a resounding crash he overturned the heavy table so that the three men were forced to jump back. From beneath his coat he withdrew the pistol from its holster.

Wine fumes blurred the trained precision with which the two officers automatically reached for their swords.

The only advantage I have, thought Edmund dully, is a clear head. These three are capable of calling on the entire neighbourhood to help apprehend me. He rocked lightly on the balls of his feet as if trying to deceive the swordsmen as to the direction in which he would make his break. In the gloom, the blades glinted malevolently.

Edmund was dimly aware that the landlord had emerged from the cellar. He stood transfixed, a jug full of wine in each hand, obviously wondering what had caused the four gentlemen to fall out. He could only hope that they would reimburse him for any damage.

Raoul lunged forward, shouting, "I'm going to kill you, English dog!"

But Edmund was lighter, swifter, and sober. He

deflected the sword with the barrel of his pistol so that it clashed against the blade held by Captain le Corde. Momentarily, their swords were all but entangled, and the two officers swore violently. This gave Edmund just sufficient time to push past, thrusting them together so that their balance was upset.

Leaning heavily on his stick, François St. Estèphe reached a hand into his pocket for a firearm. "Oh no, you don't, my fine gentleman," Edmund muttered as he dashed past, and managed to grab the walking-stick, trusting that all the man's efforts must concentrate on staying upright.

"Monsieur –" the landlord stepped forward as if to bar the young gentleman's headlong flight.

"This is no time for niceties, old fellow! I have no quarrel with you, but . . ." said Edmund, and with the stick sent both jugs flying. Behind him he heard the splintering of broken crockery and the landlord's furious oaths. Wrenching the door open, Edmund shrugged off the greatcoat that impeded his movements and left it lying in his wake together with the stick.

He did not look back, but heard the General shout, "Give me your shooter, Uncle. I can make better use of it than you."

After the obscurity within the Red Horse the daylight seemed dazzling and made Edmund blink. The breeze from the estuary caught at his nostrils. It smelt of damp, salt, and boats. The air was grey and misted with fine rain, which blotted out distance, so that the river might just as well have been open sea, for there was no sign of an opposite bank.

There was little noise out of doors apart from the scream of seabirds and the chink of harnesses as the three horses, hitched to a wooden post, moved restlessly. Their ears twitched expectantly when they saw the running man.

The narrow village street was empty. At that hour the menfolk, fishermen and wild-fowlers, were at work. The clatter of feet on cobbles brought women to the doorways, with children clutching excitedly at their skirts. As soon as they realised the strangers were intent on fighting, doors were quickly bolted.

Edmund could hear boots hammering after him. He turned, and without taking careful aim, fired his pistol. There was a brilliant flash, an ear-shattering explosion, and the acrid smell of powder. Men were cursing and screaming, but he had no time to discover if he had in fact injured anyone.

The straggle of cottages soon gave way to open country and the cobblestones became a churned-up mud track. I must find a hiding-place . . . I must find a hiding-place . . . the words resounded in his brain in unison with the pounding of his heart.

His lungs felt as if they must burst if he kept up this killing pace, and his eye-sockets seemed to burn. It was fortunate that in their haste the pursuers had not bothered to collect their horses, or else they could have easily outdistanced him. But how long would it be before they recollected, and returned for their mounts? Not long, Edmund suspected.

The bullet's whine and crack sounded curiously sharp on the moist air. Something hit Edmund's shoulder. Its impact made him stagger forward so that he all but fell in the mire. He reached his right hand across to the shoulder and recognised the warm stickiness of blood. He had been shot – no doubt, by the future Marshal. How bad the wound was Edmund could not divine, but desperation dulled the pain.

As he stumbled onwards the blood trickled down his back to mingle with his sweat. Edmund ground his teeth in fury. To have come this far with such momentous information, only to be winged by a drunken roisterer, because a French spy had evaded execution, was too impossible a coincidence.

Yet escape to England remained uppermost in his mind. There was gold aplenty in the belt around his waist, more than enough to buy him a passage across the sea and the silence of a boatman. However, in order to make contact with someone owning a craft he must not stray too far from the shore, where there was little or no cover for a fugitive.

The track wound along beside the estuary which widened towards the Channel. Edmund glanced wildly from left to right. The left was useless – open water. On the right, the countryside was strangely reminiscent of the Romney Marsh where his last desperate battle with Francis Stephens, or rather François St. Estèphe, had been joined. Flat, green marshland interlaced with treacherous ditches, but without even a solitary bush to hide him.

I'm trapped, he thought heavily, trapped like a fox who cannot reach its earth, and knows the hounds and the riders must catch up at any moment. No chance of escape. No other scent for them to pursue in error.

The mist swirled to alter its consistency so that in some places it was suddenly denser, but in others thinner showing the distance as if through gauzy curtains. That was how Edmund glimpsed the dark brake of trees growing against what looked like a gentle upland.

If he could get that far, he might be able to hide out until nightfall. Under cover of darkness he would be able to double back and seek a boatman.

To the right, the ground was lush and green but the going was heavy and difficult. Edmund prayed that he would not blunder straight into some quagmire, and skirted those patches that seemed of brightest hue. The pursuers were no longer to be heard. He deduced that they had gone for their horses and assistance. After all, they were virtually in the position to summon up an entire regiment to track him down. Nor will I be very hard to find, he thought ruefully, as startled waterfowl rose, squawking loudly, in his path.

He could hear his own agonised rasping breaths. Never before had he felt so weak, but never before had he run so hard or lost so much blood.

Just let me get to the trees, he muttered to himself, then I shall be able to rest. His lips were burning and cracked. He licked at the damp mist hoping to cool them, but it tasted salt and only increased his terrible thirst.

At last, when he feared heart and lungs would collapse under the strain, Edmund came to the shadow of the tall pines. The going became firmer and led gently uphill. He blundered on through the mysterious shadows, not even thinking what lay ahead. The tang of the sea was mixed with the spicy aroma of conifer, and Edmund longed to throw himself down on the carpet of pine needles, and catch his breath, and sleep . . .

Then he realised that the trees were opening out. Curiosity impelled him forward. He stood quite still, wondering if his wound had made him lightheaded, and if this view was a mirage borne on the wings of fever.

The forest acted as a natural wall. Beyond it in a dip lay a parkland, with formal walks, and beautifully tended flowerbeds. At its centre was a gleaming lake.

Reflected in the waters was a fairytale vision: the four elegant towers of an old château. The castle was not large, and must have been designed for beauty and pleasure rather than as a fortress, for its aura conveyed tranquillity without a hint of menace. It stood on an island quite close to the shore, so that on one side its cliff-like walls plunged straight down into the water, while the other was joined to the mainland by a humped bridge ornamented with little silvery turrets.

It was silent and perfect.

Edmund could detect no movement at any window or in the grounds. His battered spirits began to revive a little. The owners of this dream castle must be far away in Paris. He could not seek a more ideal hideaway.

On the fringe of the trees, on that side of the lake furthest from the château, stood a pretty marble rotunda. A sweet conceit where once ladies, with powdered hair and paniered brocade gowns, aped the style of tragic Marie Antoinette, and sat drinking chocolate, gossiping and reading verse. Nobody would think of searching there for an English spy.

It was chill within the little circular summer-house, but there were threadbare cushions heaped on the seats built into the walls. Edmund sank down, gasping for air. He needed water, and now the pain broke through with a dreadful vengeance. His body was wracked with uncontrollable spasms of shivering and yet he felt burning hot as if his head contained a furnace.

A strange darkness kept threatening to overwhelm his sight, as if a ring of shadow was fast enveloping him. He looked towards the castle, and thought, it is just like that old French fairytale I used to read to Serena. In there is a beautiful princess, imprisoned by an evil enchantment. Only the kiss of a valiant and handsome prince can release her from a hundred years of sleep. He smiled vaguely and closed his eyes.

I am going to die, and in a foreign land. But the awareness did not make him sad. He was too tired to struggle. Farewell, Serena, sweet sister, you will never know that you were the last person in my mind and heart before I set out on this final adventure.

The young man collapsed, his inert body sliding down on to the patterned marble floor, to look like a crumpled, discarded, life-sized marionette.

CHAPTER
THREE

ABBEVILLE was the biggest town in the area, and so its
authorities had no alternative but to obey the instructions sent by General Raoul St. Estèphe, that the
church bells be rung to warn the surrounding countryside of the English spy who was on the run. A few
village churches followed this noisy example without
anyone understanding the reason. Of course, the town
people knew why the bells sounded, but for those who
dwelt in the hamlets on the marsh and along the estuary
the cause was a mystery.

The distant clanging reached the Château d'Argent,
but its occupants were none the wiser until Raoul's
batman came with the news. To Monsieur St. Estèphe,
he announced breathlessly that the General, Captain le
Corde and Monsieur François St. Estèphe had been
delayed in a fight with a ruffian of an English spy, and
the countryside was being alerted of this danger. It was
the general's express order that all should be on their
guard.

Raoul's father smiled benignly, and said, "If my son
is in charge of this operation we have nothing to fear.
This is the last place an English desperado would
choose to visit. Go to the kitchens and you will be given
refreshment. You must need something to lay the dust
in your throat after your ride."

Using the new excitement as cover, Sophie, followed

by Vit, made towards a side door which led on to the terrace and thence across the bridge into the gardens.

"Sophie! Sophie!" Madame St. Estèphe called peevishly, "What can the girl be thinking of? Raoul will be here soon. You must make yourself pretty to greet him. You really should do something about all that hair – it is not fitting to wear it tied back like some peasant girl."

"You would not have me welcome your son wearing a frown from a headache," Sophie replied diplomatically. "The fresh air will soon chase it away."

"But there is a dangerous man in the area," Marie reminded her. "You should not go out alone."

"Vit is with me, and you are always saying he is too fierce to allow anyone to come within a yard of me."

This was undeniable, since the dog bared its yellowish teeth at whoever approached his goddess, only assuming a docile attitude on Sophie's bidding.

As she went out, Sophie heard Marie remark, "Mamma, it is her upbringing among all those dreadful fisherfolk which makes her for ever want to be running out of doors. I'm sure Raoul will put an end to that hoydenish behaviour. No, of course I'm not going to accompany her, Papa. The damp plays havoc with my hair and complexion."

The sky was a low, grey mist, pressing downwards as if trying to flatten those who trod the earth. Despite this oppressive atmosphere, it was still better to be out than enmeshed in the prattle and insinuations of Marie and her mother. Vit stood motionless for a moment, sniffing the air, his ears pricked, and then bounded as joyously as an old dog could towards the bridge.

In the soft light the château's reflection on the lake's rippling surface seemed unreal – conjured from the mist – perhaps to disappear at the blink of an eyelid.

Once across the bridge, Sophie skirted the driveway, and made instead for the paved walks edged by box hedges cut into the shapes of fantastic birds and beasts. The air was sweet with roses and mignonette. Sophie gave a sigh of relief. Here, at least, the occupants of the house would have great difficulty in following her movements. She knew without looking up at the castle that at some window Marie would be stationed, watching her every action in order to report back to Raoul.

A small smile crossed Sophie's face. What a pity that Marie could not discover some heinous fault in her behaviour, which, if told to Raoul, would completely end the possibility of marriage. But there was no chance of that. Whatever she did, Raoul would still marry her, for it was the Emperor's wish as well as the direct route to becoming a Marshal. No, she comprehended, Marie merely wished to expose some misdemeanour for which she would be scolded or punished.

Beyond the formal gardens the park unrolled like a vast carpet of springy, green turf. It was dotted with towering elms from which came the raucous complaints of rooks. At sunrise, a sharp eye might detect a herd of graceful red deer grazing here, disappearing into the forest as soon as people stirred. Save for Sophie and the dog, the grounds were quite deserted, but nonetheless they were alive with sound. A thrush had begun to trill a wild song as if it rejoiced at the passing of the storm, and although the rain had ceased to fall moisture incessantly pattered down from flowers, bushes and trees. The parkland eventually ended in a pine forest, which bordered the entire estate. On the other side of that was open terrain, marshes, the Somme Estuary, and then the open sea.

It crossed Sophie's mind, as it did each time she came

out into the gardens, that it would be comparatively easy for her to flee. Yet, where could she go without money or friends to assist her? Even if she could find her way back to the village in Brittany the St. Estèphes would flush her out, and Léontine and her relatives would be made to suffer for aiding the Emperor's jewel to escape their clutches.

Vit shambled off to snuffle among the pine trees. Poor old dog, she thought despondently, when I am no longer my own mistress, what will be your fate?

The dog seemed to find the border of the woods extraordinarily interesting. He began sniffing the ground with blind concentration, as if following up a particular scent, and headed towards the summer-house. No doubt, a rabbit or a fox had earlier run that way.

"Vit!" Sophie called sharply. For once, he was deaf to her command, and all but leaped into the rotunda. She was amazed and then alarmed to hear his sudden yelp. Thinking the dog must be hurt, she picked up her skirts, vaguely aware that they, her kid slippers and pink silk stockings were saturated. She raced across the short grass and breathlessly climbed the shallow marble steps leading into the summerhouse.

In the arched entrance Sophie stopped, and had to narrow her eyes in order to see against the gloom. Vit was standing motionless, whining softly, beside a prone body. She tiptoed closer, her heartbeats racing, and realised that the figure belonged to a young man. Even in that dull light his blond hair shone like pale gold.

Sophie knelt down. Never before had she seen a man's face possessed of more regular beauty. The mouth was wide and generous, but fine-etched, and the high-bridged nose was delicately moulded. Like soft golden fringes his long eyelashes lay still against high ivory cheekbones. She noticed the pool of blood, and from his awkward position and apparent lack of breathing had no alternative but to conclude he was dead.

"He is dead, Vit," she whispered. It was not the first time Sophie had been in the solemn presence of death, and so she felt not fear but pity and curiosity.

"I wonder who he was and how he came to be here? He has suffered dreadfully." Even in these circumstances it did not seem odd for Sophie to be talking to Vit. "His clothes are very rough and dirty, and yet I'd vow he was a gentleman. Look, how delicate are his hands."

Oblivious of the cold damp floor, Sophie continued to kneel there, one hand supporting her chin, the other reaching out to touch the man's chill forehead. She was glad his eyes were closed, but could not help wondering what colour they were. Soon, she must return to the house and inform Monsieur St. Estèphe of this tragedy, but Sophie was in no hurry.

The sun had begun to pierce the grey mist, driving it away to reveal the deep blue heavens beneath. A shaft of light found its way into the summerhouse and shone on Sophie so that she resembled a painting of a young Madonna beloved by a much earlier generation of artists.

This then is death, Edmund reflected, but I had thought it would be free of pain. My whole body still hurts damnably. He opened his eyes and was dazzled by the vision that met them. A creature of such radiance whose cloud of golden hair seemed like a halo, the wide smoky eyes bright with sadness, the skin with the softness of one of those white rose-petals that are very faintly stained with pink.

"An angel!" he murmured in English.

Sophie's hand started away from the "dead" man's head, and flew to join the other at her mouth. The stranger was alive. His eyes, even in their pain-shadowed sockets, were a clear blue.

"An angel," Edmund repeated dreamily. "If this is Heaven I shall not mind the pain while my eyes may feast on such loveliness."

Sophie assumed the man was feverish, but even that could not explain how he came to speak in a foreign tongue. He smiled up at her, and she was aware that his face, despite being streaked with dirt from the floor and lined with pain, was even more splendid than in repose.

Speaking slowly as if to a little child, Sophie hoped to make him understand. "Monsieur, if you will tell me the name of your friends and where they live, I shall get a message to them saying you are hurt but will receive the best of care. I shall go back to the château and bring help. Your wound needs a doctor's skill."

Edmund's brow creased. He blinked as he tried to concentrate his thoughts. He had not realised angels spoke in French. This one apparently did. Then, he remembered everything.

France.

This was not death but, once it was known who he was, that fate he had so narrowly escaped would certainly catch up with him. While she goes for help, he thought, I must get away. He tried to drag himself up into a sitting position. It was too painful and quite impossible. A faint groan forced itself between his clenched teeth and Edmund slumped back on to the hard floor.

Vit, who had been carefully watching his mistress

and the stranger, thumped his tail encouragingly, and then licked the man's cheek.

Sophie was amazed. True, Vit was gentle enough with small children, but he had not displayed this sort of sympathy for anyone save herself, and certainly never towards a male. Edmund put out a trembling hand and patted the dog's massive head. Vit accepted this caress graciously, and without his customary warning snarl.

"Good dog," Edmund said in French. "You look fiercer than you are. A lamb disguised as Cerberus!"

"Ah, you speak French!" Sophie was overjoyed, and the pleasure bubbled in her voice. A brilliant smile lit up her features, and Edmund was instantly reminded of a flower opening its beauty to the sun. How dreadful it would have been, thought Sophie, if this gentleman was not able to converse with me; for she had already resolved that it must be her duty to nurse him at the château and she dismissed from her mind any opposition from the St. Estèphes. "Vit is not usually so tolerant of strangers, monsieur. He regards me as a property to be guarded with fierce growls and bared teeth, but he seems to have taken to you. Now, please tell me your name so I may know who I am helping?"

How wonderful, Edmund mused with relief, her voice matches her face. Some beauties had destroyed themselves utterly in his eyes and ears the moment they opened their pretty mouths to emit nothing but shrill inanities. Dare I tell her the truth? he wondered stupidly. No, of course not. She is a Frenchwoman, and however beautiful her face, soft her voice and gentle her manner, she must be filled with revulsion and fury on learning who and what I am. There will be no mercy even from her.

He closed his eyes.

Alarmed, Sophie leaned closer. He heard the rustling of her gown and inhaled the fresh scent issuing from her warmth, for Léontine always strewed lavender in her lady's linen, and Sophie used verbena and rosemary in her washing water to keep her complexion smooth, blemish-free, and sweet-smelling.

"Ah, monsieur, please come back to me. Don't die," the sweet voice entreated, throbbing with emotion.

"And who could refuse you anything, madame?" Edmund responded feebly, without opening his eyes.

"Mademoiselle," she corrected him primly.

And Edmund felt inexplicably relieved.

"This is no time for gallantry," Sophie reproved, blushing a little, and added coaxingly, "If you are strong enough for that you are surely able to tell me your name."

"I have no choice," he said. "My name is Edmund Apsley."

The name Apsley was awkward to her tongue, and she had to say it several times before achieving a passable version. Edmund was easier since she pronounced it the French way, "Edmond". "Edmond. Edmond," she repeated.

"I do not think I have ever heard it spoken so charmingly," the owner of that name commented.

Sophie gave his forehead a gentle tap to warn him not to say such things, and asked, "But, what country is yours, Monsieur Ap . . . Apsley?"

"Mademoiselle," he returned with all the formality he could muster in his parlous state, "I regret to have to tell *you* I am an Englishman."

Her smoke-grey eyes grew huge with alarm. English! Was not the devil an Englishman? She was sure Léontine had told her as much. The enemy. No woman was safe with an Englishman. They were monsters who ate nothing but roast beef and plum pudding, and drank strong ale. She thought they had red faces and fat bellies, but was not sure how widespread was this image. The stranger seemed possessed of neither the appearance nor the habits of the dreadful English. She cast Vit a reproachful glance. His judgement was ill-founded this time. How could he of all creatures trust the enemy?

Then realisation flooded into her mind. "You are the spy they are all seeking," she stated gravely.

He did not deny it. "I was on my way back to England, when I had the misfortune to be recognised by someone. One of your soldiers managed to shoot me. No ordinary fellow, but a general, and by all accounts, a future Marshal of France . . . General St. Estèphe."

"General St. Estèphe?" she echoed.

"Do you know him?" Even in his weak condition Edmund was astonished at the coincidence.

"Very little," she said stiffly. "But we are to be betrothed tomorrow." Her voice caught a little as she continued, "And married very soon . . ."

"Great Heaven!" Edmund's mind seemed to explode. What had that drunken sot called this miracle of beauty? "A virginal little doll"? Why had he not taken the opportunity there and then to horsewhip the fellow? That this angel should become the man's wife was as repugnant as any fairytale of Beauty and the Beast, but he doubted even the little mademoiselle's sweetness could transform the red-faced general into a handsome and desirable prince.

'But you should not be here," Sophie said. "He is coming at any moment –"

"This is your home?"

She shook her head, and raised her chin defiantly. "Not any more, Monsieur Englishman. I was born here, yes, but then came the Revolution. My parents, Comte and Comtesse de Fontenoy, were brutally murdered on the denunciation of some of the people from their estates, whose name was St. Estèphe." She paused to see if he understood, but Edmund's eyes, despite the pain, were dark with sympathy and realisation.

"And you, Mademoiselle de Fontenoy?" he asked gently.

"My nurse, Léontine, took me to her family – simple fishing people in Brittany – who cared for me as their own. But, then she brought me back to Paris, for she said I must lead a life more fitting for a de Fontenoy."

"And is it suitable for one of your name to wed one of theirs?" he demanded fiercely.

"The Emperor has commanded it," she said stiffly. "I have no choice in the matter. This way my children . . ." she stumbled over the word, "will own what would once have been theirs by the right of inheritance."

"His children," Edmund reminded her, and discovered the very idea made his stomach churn with disgust.

The wonderful grey eyes became tempest-tossed oceans. "Do you imagine *I* desire this marriage?" Sophie cried, and all the bitterness she had suppressed since the Emperor's command was first made known to her welled up in that question. "I have no family to speak for me. No one who cares for me, save old Léontine. And the powerful do not listen to such as she. I am nothing but the Emperor's trinket, to be bestowed where he deems most fit . . ."

There was compassion in Edmund's eyes. Somehow this, his helplessness, and his duplicity enraged Sophie the more. Dead, he had been the handsome stranger whose passing she must mourn, and around whom she was free to spin fantasies. Alive, he was almost the prince of chivalry in one of her fairytales, wounded but still valiant and trustworthy. The truth had destroyed that image. Sophie knew it was unreasonable to blame Edmund Apsley for being who he was, and so disappointing her . . . but she still did.

"You, Englishman, have no right to pity me," Sophie said defiantly. "I am to be a great lady. Yes, *Madame la Maréchale* herself. The friend of Napoleon and Josephine. A constant visitor to their court. A lady of rank and fashion. While you . . . you will die as you deserve . . ."

This knowledge so horrified her that the tears began to course down her cheeks, so that Vit, whimpering with sympathy, pushed his nose against her face as if trying to staunch their flow. He gave the stranger one reproachful look for causing all this trouble.

"You are quite right, mademoiselle," Edmund agreed. "Forgive me for intruding where I have no place. Now, may I advise you as to what would be best for you. Go at once to the château and inform General St. Estèphe and Monsieur François St. Estèphe that you have caught his English spy. Matters will be taken out of your fair hands. You will even gain prestige . . ."

She gazed at him through her tears. His jaw was set as firm as carved ivory, and she understood he spoke only for her good. "Why, oh, why, did you come here, Englishman?" she asked brokenly. "I do not want your blood on my conscience."

"If I had known that I must bring grief into your

gentle heart," Edmund returned softly, "I would rather have died a thousand times somewhere back there. But, Mademoiselle de Fontenoy, I can never regret coming here, however long I survive, for I shall die knowing I have gazed on the fairest woman earth possesses."

"No!" Sophie's use of that one word contained a rebellion and strength she never knew were hers. "You will not die like that, Monsieur . . . Edmond . . . ah, the Ap . . . Apsley is too difficult. I cannot permit it. I will tend your wound, and bring you food and drink. When you are a little stronger you can go where you please . . . to the Devil if that is where you belong. But I shall not give you up to *them*."

Edmund stared at the girl's determined expression with wonder. Before he could warn her of the hazard and foolishness of her intention, another voice broke the silence.

"You silly, silly child!" it said roughly. "You don't know what you are saying. Your heart gets in the way of your head!"

Edmund closed his eyes. Now, he was finished. The stranger's grim expression gave no hope for any chance of salvation.

Vit stood up and ambled over to the stout woman whose snuff-coloured gown was relieved by a white frilled tucker. Her wiry grey locks seemed to be trying to escape from the confines of a snowy cap. In one hand she held a basket, covered with a cloth, at which Vit began sniffing hopefully. The dog looked up at the woman and then directed his glance back to Sophie and Edmund as if he was trying to tell her something.

"Léontine!" Sophie jumped to her feet. "You have been spying on me. How long have you been here?"

"If I spy on you it is only for your protection," the other retorted. "As to how long I have been here: long enough to hear you talk treason and risk your beautiful neck for the likes of him . . ." she jerked an uncompromising thumb towards the immobile man.

"You are right, Madame," Edmund said calmly. "This lady must not be involved with me. You go back to the house and tell them . . ."

"In such a rush to die, eh, Englishman?" Léontine interrupted coldly. She squatted down beside him, and peered into his face with small brown and suspicious eyes. Taking a pair of scissors hanging from the cord at her waist, she deftly cut away the cloth on the shoulder of his jacket, and with knotted but surprisingly gentle fingers started to probe the wound.

Edmund's knuckles turned bone white as he clenched them against the pain. He looked up and saw Sophie's face, pale and anxious, framed in the glorious cloud of golden hair which had become free of its ribbon. He tried to smile reassuringly through his dry lips.

"Fortunately for you, Englishman, it is only a flesh wound. The bullet has not lodged there. The Devil certainly takes care of his own, as we say."

Edmund gave a lop-sided grin. "I am so thirsty, Madame, can you not give me a mouthful of water?" he implored.

"I can do better than that," she returned roughly. "Mademoiselle Sophie, in the basket there is some wine. I brought you a little repast. You have eaten nothing all day and will faint with hunger and fatigue if you go on like that. You, naughty girl . . ."

Even though his mind was clouded with pain Edmund recognised that the scolding masked an overwhelming love.

Eagerly, Sophie took out a flask of red wine. Ignoring Léontine's outstretched hand, she knelt down again beside Edmund and held the bottle to his lips. Once again he inhaled her intoxicating perfume, and felt her silken tresses brush against his cheek.

"That will give you some strength, Englishman," she said. "You have lost a lot of blood."

The wine was strong and sour. It brought warmth to Edmund's limbs but made his head feel light and almost carefree. He gazed at the two women who seemed to combine all the aspects he most admired in womanhood: indomitable strength, courage, skill, gentleness, beauty and self-sacrifice.

"It is time for me to speak," Léontine said gruffly. "No," she held up a hand to silence Sophie. "Mademoiselle, you must listen too. Know this, Monsieur Englishman, I would lay down my life for this child rather than let any harm befall her. When she went out for her walk with the dog I waited, and then followed to make sure she needed nothing –"

"Léontine," Sophie interrupted, "I am not a little girl now . . ."

"Hush, child. I do not know about the English," the woman continued gravely, "except they have barbarous eating habits, but they do not guillotine their king and queen and noble families, so I do not think they are entirely bad . . ."

Edmund was going to tell her of the execution of Charles I, but the wine had made him too drowsy to embark on a history lesson.

"The St. Estèphes!" She spat delicately on the marble floor. "They are worse than the English, and while I cannot rescue my little lady from them I do not have to help them win more honour and glory by capturing a helpless Englishman that my foolish child wishes to shield."

"You mean you won't tell *them*," Sophie smiled with relief.

"Of course not." Léontine sounded irritated.

"Madame . . ." began Edmund, and tried to shake the woman's rough, work-reddened hand.

"Do not thank me," she muttered, "thank her. But, remember this, Monsieur Englishman, if ever you harm a hair of her head I shall kill you more surely than the general."

"I am glad to know that," Edmund said solemnly. Léontine shot him one of her shrewd, closed looks as if searching behind his words.

"But we must fetch him food, clothing, and bandages . . . and his wound must be washed and treated . . ." Sophie insisted.

"First, we must get him to safety," said Léontine. "He cannot stay here. It will not be long before someone comes here on some pretext or other. Besides, he will die if he does not sleep indoors. He already has a fever." She passed the back of her hand across Edmund's burning forehead, and nodded to herself.

"But where can we hide him?" Sophie demanded.

"With the charcoal-burners in the forest," Léontine replied, and turned to Edmund to explain: "I have known these people since before the little lady was born. They have always had a settlement in the de Fontenoy forests. Their huts are not very elegant, monsieur, or particularly clean, but you will be safe. They are good folk, and do not trouble themselves with laws or politics, or whether people are powerful and rich. They will see you need help, and you will receive it, especially as the daughter of the de Fontenoys wishes it.

I shall fetch one of them to carry you into the forest. He will be brawny enough to bear even an Englishman. But, Mademoiselle Sophie, you must go back to the château immediately."

"Oh, let me stay here with Monsieur Edmond, while you go for help. He must not be left alone."

"No. Vit will stand guard here if you tell him. You must not be absent when General St. Estèphe, Captain le Corde and François arrive."

"But . . ." Sophie objected.

"They will come looking for you," the woman reasoned. "Do you want that – while *he* is still here?"

"No."

"Then do as I suggest."

"Shall I see him again?"

"I imagine so," the woman replied cryptically.

Sophie leaned close to Edmund. "You have nothing to fear now," she said earnestly. "Léontine's friends will never betray you. And," her smile was mischievous, so that for the first time he noticed there was a small, enchanting dimple in her chin, "you will learn that her bark is a good deal worse than her bite . . . like Vit."

"I am glad you have two watchdogs," murmured Edmund. "When next shall I see you?"

"Very soon, if that is what you want," came the demure response. "Until then, Monsieur Edmond, I wish you well, and I do thank you for . . . for caring what happens to me."

Edmund took the proffered hand as if it were the most precious treasure of any century. "Thank you, Mademoiselle de Fontenoy, for giving me my life."

It was Léontine who broke the strange spell. Gruffly, she ordered: "Mademoiselle Sophie, will you please be

gone! Vit, stay here! Monsieur, you finish the wine.
There is a cold chicken and a little raspberry tart in the
basket, but I doubt whether you are strong enough to
take solid victuals. I shall be away for ten minutes at the
most. Be calm till I return."

When she reached the entrance to the summerhouse,
Sophie hesitated and looked back at the man beside
whom Vit stood like a sentinel, ears pricked, nose
quivering, tail quite still. Edmund's last glimpse of her
was of a slender, ethereal figure, with a cascade of
golden hair, etched against the sunlit gardens. He
closed his eyes, and sank into a deep swoon, so he did
not hear Léontine's parting words:

"Englishman, I fear you have brought us more prob-
lems than we can hope to solve . . ."

CHAPTER
FOUR

So that her appearance would not disgrace them at the
betrothal ball, the St. Estèphes had graciously lent
Sophie some of the jewels that had belonged to the
Comtesse de Fontenoy. How could the fiancée of General Raoul St. Estèphe, a future Marshal of France,
greet the Emperor and Empress with no finery save the
imperial gift?

If Edmund Apsley had considered Sophie a vision of
beauty in her crumpled gown and unbound hair, he
would have been dazzled by her betrothal array.

Indeed, as she gazed at what seemed a remote and
splendid stranger in her looking-glass, Sophie could not
resist wondering what Monsieur the Englishman would
think of her. Her heart knew an unaccountable sadness
that he might never see her like this, and Sophie was
half angry with herself for such silly regrets. A gentleman in his dubious profession would have been entangled with so many beautiful and fashionable females, he
would hardly be aware of a girl who, for the first time in
her life, wore all the trappings of luxury. Besides, was it
not treachery to care about the opinion of an English
spy?

Until that evening the St. Estèphes had regarded
costly apparel an unnecessary extravagance for
Mademoiselle de Fontenoy. Time enough for that
when she was wife of the Marshal. But a celebration

attended by the Emperor and Empress in their own château warranted some money being spent even on a chit who had once gone barefoot with her skirts above her ankles like any common fishergirl! They could not have Napoleon thinking they did not treasure his jewel.

So this was the first gown Leroy had created for Sophie. It was magnificent, for the great designer had declared that to dress one of such youth and slenderness gave him the sort of inspiration that could not be found from the whims of rich, fading Parisians, with their enamelled skins, dyed tresses and overblown figures. He had mentioned this within earshot of Marie Le Corde which had deepened her disagreeable expression, and her envy and dislike of the girl who was shortly to become her sister-in-law.

Following the dictates of current styles, the gown had a high waist and low décolletage, but it could not be dismissed as just one more elegant robe. The overdress with its short train was fashioned from cloth of silver that opened just beneath the bosom to reveal spangled white tulle matching the small puffed sleeves. On Sophie's supple form these glittering fabrics were neither stiff nor constricting, but with each movement she seemed to be clad in a beam of moonlight.

Léontine had lovingly rinsed Sophie's hair in water in which camomile flowers had been steeped. After brushing it a couple of hundred times she had divided the tresses in order to polish them with a piece of silk until they gleamed like skeins of pure gold. Then she had arranged the hair so that a waterfall of lustrous curls bobbed against the girl's delicate neck and kissed her soft cheeks. No ornament disturbed the style, which was not the latest, but its effect was too exquisite to need the constraint of any transient fashionable fad.

On Sophie's little wrists were placed the once-renowned de Fontenoy pearl and diamond bracelets – now owned by Madame St. Estèphe – and in her ears glinted matching earrings. The final touch was the Emperor's gift: it was pinned to her bodice at the cleft of her small bosom, and everyone agreed this lent the final touch of elegance.

Marie le Corde regarded Sophie's completed toilette with hot, jealous eyes, and bit her lips so that the rouge on them cracked. Now she could wish she had chosen silver instead of green and gold. Madame St. Estèphe, tightly corseted, so that her Grecian gown could flow unhindered by fleshy bulges, was delighted with the appearance of her future daughter-in-law, but could not help wishing her own dear Marie was not so thoroughly eclipsed by this young nobody. Perhaps the green with gold was a little too garish. It set off her own violet tulle, to be sure, but then neither of their gowns, although they had cost more, had the charm of Sophie's . . .

"So you are a normal young female after all. I had begun to wonder, hadn't you, Marie?" grumbled Madame St. Estèphe, much relieved to see a small dreamy smile play on Sophie's lips. "After all that this is costing us it would have been a crime for you to attend your betrothal ball with a countenance borrowed from a funeral. I am pleased you are looking forward to opening the dancing with my Raoul . . ."

But, the fond Mamma was quite wrong. The reason for Sophie's expression was scarcely anticipation but memory . . . a memory that heightened her colour, quickened her pulse and seemed to steal the ground from beneath her feet.

She had coaxed a protesting Léontine into going out in the early dawn to gather an armful of herbs which would be beneficial to the wounded and debilitated. Safe in the knowledge that Raoul's Mamma and sister would be indulging in a particularly late beauty sleep that morning, Sophie had slipped out into the grounds.

Of course Léontine had tried to deter her from going. "But I must visit him, dear one," Sophie had insisted gravely. "Everything in this basket will aid his recovery. That wound must be cleaned and anointed without more delay. I shall not be unprotected. Vit will accompany me."

Sophie did not admit to her old nurse that she also wished to see Edmund Apsley again to ensure that he was as handsome as she remembered.

And, almost as if to keep this thought at bay, she hurried through the woodland, reminding herself aloud of each of the remedies she had concocted for the Englishman.

Sophie had learned plant-lore as a little girl in the humble community that had no other medicinal resources than those plucked from the hedgerow or grown in a patch of earth beside a tumbledown cottage. Little had she imagined this wisdom learned in childhood would ever again be needed or could stand her in such good stead now she was an adult.

The small knot of men whose blackened face proclaimed to the world their particular calling had nodded politely but incuriously when the young woman and large dog appeared in their clearing. Only one of them, a huge stooped giant, had come forward.

"I am Jaconnet," he had mumbled, shyly ducking his head. "The wounded one is in my hut, and he is not doing so well this morning. I am pleased that you have come, for I cannot tell what is best for him."

Sophie had commanded the dog to remain outside the hut on guard. It took a while for her eyes to grow accustomed to the gloom indoors, but she could not fail to recognise the glitter of fever in Edmund Apsley's gaze. He was lying on a palliasse thrashing about as if his body was trying to break free of the wound which shackled it.

"I shall need lots of hot clean water . . ."

Without a word, Jaconnet had gone out to return within a few seconds bearing a bubbling cauldron. Then he left Sophie alone with the Englishman.

Beneath her cool hand the man's forehead seemed to exude the heat of a blacksmith's furnace. "I thought you only existed in my dreams," he whispered. His brief smile told Sophie that he was even more handsome than her memory of him.

"Hush now, Monsieur Edmond," she said firmly. "You must husband your strength while I attend to this wound."

His eyes followed her small, deft movements as she unpacked the basket, and set out strips of clean linen, pots of unguent and neat bunches of greenery. She examined the earthenware drinking-bowl beside him, and finding it contained a few dregs of apple brandy, shook her head disapprovingly. "I daresay good Jaconnet gave it to you to dull the pain and make you sleep, but it won't help the fever. Now, to please me you will drink this, which will."

She rinsed the bowl, filled it with hot water and added a handful of box leaves. Obediently Edmund swallowed the liquid, while the girl began unbuttoning his shirt. Her golden tresses caressed his burning face, and once again he inhaled the perfume he had believed part of his dreams. "I would cheerfully be put to the most agonising torture, Mademoiselle de Fontenoy, if you were close beside me," he murmured.

The shadows concealed the blush that stained Sophie's cheeks, but she countered primly, "If I were there, monsieur, I should not permit anyone to maltreat you."

The linen shirt was caked with dried blood. Beneath it, Jaconnet had placed some none-too-clean rags to staunch the bleeding. As Sophie pulled these away, Edmund uttered a small cry, and her own eyes glistened in sympathy. "The quicker I am the sooner will you be comfortable. You have my word."

She dipped a piece of linen in the boiling water, and began to clean the wound on the muscular, fair-skinned shoulder. The man bit his lips against the pain and finished drinking the potion of box.

Once the blood was washed away Sophie could see clearly the jagged wound left by the bullet. "You lead a charmed life, Monsieur Englishman," she remarked softly. "Another centimetre and the bullet would have been lodged to do you great damage. Now there is good use for Jaconnet's spirit. I am afraid this will hurt you, but there can be no surer cleanser."

She picked up the blackened, greasy leather bottle that reeked of apple brandy and sprinkled some of this on to a cloth which she held firmly against his flesh.

Edmund gave a faint cry, tensed his body and closed his eyes. "By Heaven, mademoiselle," he gasped, "I don't care to think what this stuff does to a man's stomach if that's how it affects his flesh."

Sophie uttered a small gurgling laugh. "You will do

very well, Englishman, if you can muster a jest at such a moment. Now, here is something much less painful." She removed the cloth and in its place applied a paste of comfrey, and then dressed the wound with strips of linen.

"How neat you are," Edmund said admiringly. "I did not know young ladies could be possessed of such skill and courage." He paused as if some new thought had entered his mind. "But then I have never met one quite like you – a blend of ethereal princess and practical countrywoman."

Although Sophie rejoiced at this compliment she could not help wondering again just how many girls he had known . . . and loved.

"Who could imagine a bullet might bring a man such good fortune," Edmund continued. "If such comforts were promised to all, men would be fighting each other merely for the pleasure of being wounded."

"Enough of your gallantry," Sophie chided him. "You need your strength and plenty of sleep. I am leaving some simples here and shall explain to Jaconnet the best time for you to be given them. Do not refuse these medicines or whatever he offers you to eat if you want to grow strong enough to leave these shores without delay."

"Now I have set eyes on you, mademoiselle, I begin to wonder if I ever wish to depart," the Englishman murmured dreamily.

"That is your fever speaking rather than common sense." This calm pronouncement belied Sophie's quickly beating heart. His speeches are mere dalliance such as all handsome gentlemen indulge in, her brain reminded that heart sternly. The heart remained obstinately unconvinced.

"You will return soon?" There was pleading in the Englishman's voice.

"Naturally. I have to ensure my patient is taking the medicines I have prescribed," she said smiling. "I promise to return sometime tomorrow. Here's my hand on it."

Sophie held out her small white hand, and he noticed how its delicacy was tempered by strong capability. This girl's fragility was deceptive, Edmund decided. Within her was a vein of diamond-like resolution which might well cut those who attempted to cross her deepest convictions. A rare mixture in any female, he concluded, especially one born on this side of the Channel. Experience and patriotism had taught him to suspect all French men . . . and women . . . of an innate perfidy. It was hard to believe he had stumbled upon one of their number without this flaw.

He did not accept her hand. "That is a paltry way to seal your promise."

Mystified, Sophie gazed at him. The question formed on her lips remained unuttered, for suddenly Edmund Apsley struggled into a sitting position and used his good arm to draw her down so that their faces were level and very close. Notwithstanding his loss of blood the man's grasp was exceedingly strong. Sophie realised she would have to use both her hands to push him away, and she feared any action that might aggravate the wound.

His mouth pressed hard against lips that had opened in protest. No man had ever kissed her, and Sophie was quite unprepared for the sweet intoxication which seemed to rob her senses of all reason. A cloud of warm ecstasy surrounded her and the ground beneath her feet dissolved so that she was forced to twine her arms about the Englishman's neck to keep herself from falling.

Reluctantly and very gently, Edmund withdrew his mouth, and his arm. He noted how her long fair lashes lay against the perfect curve of her bright cheeks. Her eyelids flickered open to display eyes filled with astonished happiness.

"I had heard that Englishmen are devils," she said breathlessly. "And now I know it to be true!"

Edmund produced a lazy smile which endowed his good looks with a certain roguishness. "So an angel has been embraced by one of these demons, eh, Mademoiselle Sophie?" he teased. "And I declare looks none the worse for that terrible experience. But your kiss assures me you will hold to your promise."

A brilliant blush suffused Sophie's face, rising from her slender pale throat. She backed away from him, staggering like a child taking its first steps. "After your scandalous behaviour," she said stiffly, "I certainly shan't come here alone."

"What! Do I have to embrace your old dragon of a nurse too?" Edmund jested weakly.

Deliberately, Sophie de Fontenoy turned her back on the devilish Englishman so that he saw that the flush had even invaded the nape of her neck. "Don't be foolish." To her own ears her tone sounded insufficiently stern, perhaps because her lips were twitching at the idea of Léontine being kissed by this man. Wound or no wound, he would know what it was to have his ears soundly boxed!

"You cannot make me believe you found my attentions totally unwelcome," Edmund stated an unassailable truth.

Sophie shook back her curls. "Oh, I am sure a person

who has kissed so many females must be able to divine these things," she agreed hotly.

"Precisely," Edmund smiled, and watched the girl's back stiffen.

Then there was a sudden silence. Alarmed, Sophie turned and saw he was once more lying down, eyes shut and face as pale and drawn as in death. She hastened to his side, and put a gentle hand to his brow. It was moist and cool. The fever was beginning to break.

Edmund Apsley's eyes opened, and despite the pain shadowing them, they were both merry and affectionate.

"Do you seek to seal your promise yet again?" he asked, feigning to raise himself on one elbow.

Sophie stepped away. "I merely wished to ascertain whether you were sleeping as I had advised, or in a faint. But you appear too impudent to require further attention, so I shall leave now."

"But you will come back?" he entreated.

She closed the door behind her without replying, but both of them knew how she would have answered.

Sophie started as Madame St. Estèphe's shrill voice penetrated her memories to remind her where she was and what was expected of her. The woman patted her cheek. "Dreaming of my Raoul, eh, Sophie? And no wonder, seeing he's such a handsome and amiable fellow," she continued, believing her opinion confirmed by the girl's heightened colour. "Come, girls, we must go down and show ourselves to the gentlemen before our guests arrive. I am sure they will shower us with pretty compliments."

Arm-in-arm with Marie, she led the way down the great carved stairway, with Sophie following more slowly, intent on managing her train and banishing Edmund's embrace from the forefront of her mind.

The lofty hall had been transformed from a rather cool and gloomy place. Now, it positively glittered with hundreds of candle flames reflected in an eternity of mirrors. A heady perfume filled the air from the floral decorations.

Standing in the centre of the black and white marble floor, fluted glasses of champagne clutched in their hands, the gentlemen of the house were deeply engrossed in conversation. So much so that they looked quite startled when the ladies approached, as if they had forgotten the real reason for being gathered together, or indeed why they, as well as the females, were so richly attired.

Without hearing a word exhanged, Sophie instinctively knew their talk was of the English spy. She had reason to be grateful to Edmund Apsley, for since Raoul's arrival at the Château d'Argent the previous evening he had had no time to spend with her, being too busy sending out riders to discover traces of the accursed Englishman. By now the family had been regaled with the story of the events at the Red Horse.

Prompted by the determined expression in his wife's eyes, Monsieur St. Estèphe was the first to recollect his social duties, and he came forward, exclaiming jovially, "Well, well – just look at our ladies. Now, here's a sight for sore eyes, I must say. They do look magnificent, especially you, my dear Clothilde. Violet is certain'y your colour. Why, you could be our Marie's sister, and not her mamma."

Madame St. Estèphe simpered under this rare display of gallantry.

Her brother-in-law, François, nodded briefly. He

had no time for pleasantries, for he was reiterating to his nephew his grievances against the entire English nation, in particular against Edmund Apsley.

Sophie's prettily jewelled ears picked up that name, and heard how he, and his sister, had somehow been instrumental in destroying the French spy ring.

"A more interfering baggage you can't imagine," François hissed. "If it weren't for her, and that brother . . ."

As with anything that touched on the fairer sex, Raoul could not refrain from asking idly, "Pretty?"

His uncle cast him a dark look. It was clear he did not feel the general was taking the business of the English spy seriously enough. "Her appearance was adequate, I imagine, but she was as impudent as any member of that treacherous race . . ."

So, he has a sister, mused Sophie, delighted to learn a little more about Edmund Apsley. If she knew of his work she must spend many a sleepless night worrying over his fate, and Sophie could not help wondering what sort of person was this "impudent" English-woman who had so upset François St. Estèphe's schemes.

Listening to François, Sophie began to understand just how much this man hated Edmund Apsley. It was no mere loathing for the enemy but a personal vendetta: the Englishman had cost him his master's high opinion of his abilities as an agent. In order to regain Napoleon's favour, François St. Estèphe obviously believed it necessary to be the one who apprehended the spy.

Thinking of Edmund safely asleep in old Jaconnet's hut, Sophie could feel almost lighthearted. That would be the last place Raoul's uncle would seek his quarry.

"Oh, don't fret so," the nephew chimed in, rather

vexed at the way his uncle kept harping on the English spy. "I am sure my men are bound to catch up with the scurvy villain soon. Seeing this matter means so much to you, what do you say to my ensuring that you are the first actually to lay hands on him? That ought to bring a glimmer of a smile to your countenance."

Even in so brief an acquaintanceship Sophie knew Raoul was not given to selfless acts, so she understood the fate of a solitary Englishman was relatively unimportant to him.

His uncle seemed not to have heard. "I vow by all that's sacred I shall get him," François said, and Sophie thought that if snakes possessed the power of speech they would use similarly vicious tones. "And when that devil is in my clutches he will pay dearly for what he did to me. He will certainly die." He gave one of his rare laughs – an unpleasant mirthless sound. "But not quickly . . ."

CHAPTER
FIVE

SOPHIE'S expression must have grown as chill as her body, for she felt Marie's sharp elbow in her side, and heard her whisper furiously: "At least, try to look as if you care something for him. To think my brother could have his pick of women, and all he gets is one who . . ." She did not complete her opinion of Sophie, but turned instead to her husband, demanding without much coquetry: "Well, Martin, how do you say I look, eh?"

Martin le Corde sighed before answering, and Sophie guessed he knew that whatever his reply it would be wrong, and either lead to a dispute there and then, or else be remembered and used later.

"Very grand," came the flat response.

From the way his wife glared at him, this was clearly not what she had sought.

"Now then, that's enough about the Englishman. Raoul, won't you look at your pretty little fiancée?" Monsieur St. Estèphe took Sophie firmly by the wrist, and drew her towards his son.

He was a portly old gentleman with thinning white hair, and cheeks made all the redder from tiny broken veins. Nowadays, he was more interested in filling his stomach than in politics and warfare, and it was quite difficult for Sophie to imagine that once he had led the murderous rabble which had attacked this very château. Yet his close-set eyes were similar to his son's, and she could well believe Raoul capable of such actions, or worse . . .

Raoul St. Estèphe turned reluctantly from his uncle, and his dark gaze swept mockingly over the girl who had been given him by the Emperor. Beside him, Sophie seemed even more diminutive, for Raoul was unusually tall with massive shoulders. Feeling his eyes on her, Sophie found herself wondering about the Englishman's height. It had been impossible to judge while he lay prone. Still, when he was well she would see him on his feet, and then she would know. The thought of Edmund being strong enough to walk gave Sophie pleasure, so that Raoul looked down on a girl whose lips were wistfully curving.

Of course, he mistook the meaning, and thought, so, the little virgin does not detest me. Her first expressions of loathing were intended to make me more interested, eh? She is like the rest of the petticoat brigade, and will become as eager in due course, I don't doubt.

"So, Mademoiselle Sophie, you do not hate me too badly, after all?" he said banteringly, and winked at his brother-in-law. "You look very appetising, I must say. That outfit must have cost us a pretty packet. But, damn me, if it doesn't suit you. Though myself I prefer a girl to wear brighter colours. Still, for an unmarried maiden . . ." he leered insinuatingly, and Sophie tried unsuccessfully not to blush, "white is very proper."

"Soon, she'll be able to wear the brightest of colours if such considerations still guide modern young females," his father interrupted boisterously. "I make no secret of it, Sophie, m'dear, I'm depending on you to supply me with a grandchild – make it a boy if you can – but I expect it within the first year of your marriage, so don't keep me waiting. Not like my Marie. She still shows no sign of producing a babe. Too fond of galli-vanting, aren't you, Marie? You don't fancy being tied down to a little one. Poor old Martin, I know you'd like an heir, wouldn't you?"

If indeed I do have a child before her, thought Sophie, nauseated at what must be, she will hate me even more for that.

"Yes, grandchildren is what we want from you, Sophie, eh, Clothilde?" old St. Estèphe boomed, care-fully ignoring his wife's warning shake of the head as she tried to indicate that this was not the most delicate of topics.

"If it's grandchildren you want, pa," roared his son, laughing loudly, "go on down to the village. You'll see a few shoots off the St. Estèphe tree there. I can't deny they're mine, even if I have doubts about their mother's virtue, for they look too much like I did at that age. Ask Martin, he's seen 'em, and heard the little rascals call me 'papa'."

The men guffawed at this announcement while Marie and her mother tittered behind their hands. Only Sophie could not smile. He was, she thought, utterly despicable. The fisherfolk, who often failed to put a wedding before a christening, were never so coarse in front of their women.

"Oh, Raoul," remonstrated his mother, "perhaps you should not speak so with Sophie here."

"Tut! Tut!" Raoul grinned, and unrepentantly slap-ped his satined thigh, "Have I shocked my little fian-cée? Never mind, Sophie dearest, you'll get used to my ways very soon, just as you'll fulfil Papa's legitimate ambitions." He gave another burst of ribald laughter. "It's best I tell you the truth now, then we won't have any silly arguments when we're wed.

"Anyway, you'd better give me one of your pretty smiles, for I've brought you a present. I expect that'll make you love me a little. I shall demand a kiss for it, or my name's not Raoul St. Estèphe . . ." He slid an arm around her tiny waist. Sophie tried not to draw away, but felt as if even the blood circulating in her body flinched from his touch.

"A present!" echoed Marie. "What have you brought *her*? Show us this instant."

"Don't get yourself in such a state, little sister," Raoul said coolly. "Martin gave you much the same when you two were betrothed. It's the usual basket of goodies you girls know we'll shell out before the wedding day."

"Humph," was his sister's ungracious response. "It may be the traditional gift between engaged couples, but I do think Martin could have managed something a bit better."

The General put two fingers to his mouth to produce a piercing whistle which startled the ladies.

"Raoul—" his mother began to remonstrate, but Monsieur St. Estèphe hushed her. He was clearly tickled at his son's unorthodox behaviour.

Almost immediately the General's batman entered, saluting smartly and clicking his heels, although the effect was somewhat marred by his unbuttoned tunic and bulging cheek which suggested his master had disturbed him in the middle of a meal.

"Raoul!" Marie's voice rose several notes in displeasure. "This is not a barracks. Pray act as if you've always lived in a château and require your man to behave as a proper servant . . ."

Her brother shrugged, and then roared at his man: "You idle dog! Remember, you are not off duty until I say so. Stop chewing immediately! Go and fetch those two boxes from my chamber.''

With another salute, and a hasty swallow, the man departed, and Raoul said airily, ''That's the only way to treat rankers. If you're too polite to them, they think they're as good as you and start taking liberties. I do not want them to love me, only to obey me.''

He did not notice Sophie's small ironic smile. So, it seemed the peasant who climbed to power was just as anxious to put his foot on another's neck as he had been to throw off the aristocracy's yoke.

The batman returned to deposit the baskets on two chairs. Marie and her mother rushed over to them as if these presents were intended for them. ''Do hurry up, Sophie. Open them before the guests arrive. We want to know what Raoul has brought you,'' Madame St. Estèphe urged, and her face, despite its liberal dusting of powder, began to shine with excitement.

Sophie would not have been a normal girl if she had not been curious and eager. Her heart quickened at the idea of so many surprises. Besides, unlike the St. Estèphes, she was not yet used to receiving gifts. Such luxuries were beyond the scope of fisherfolk, although there had always been flowers, or pretty shells, or even a splendid fish for her birthday, but nothing that had to be purchased, for who had money to spend?

The first basket was quite large, and shaped like a conch shell. When the spangled ribbons were untied and the wrapping papers removed Sophie could scarcely believe her eyes. There was a brilliant crimson silk gown, heavily embroidered with gold thread; an equally vivid cashmere shawl; a miniature depicting two fat cherubs and a goddess, somewhat lacking in clothes, set in a jewel-studded frame; a pair of combs encrusted with sparkling gems; and an ornate ring fashioned as a serpent with large rubies for eyes and too large even to fit one of her thumbs.

Wonderingly, Sophie lifted out each item to the appreciative gasps of Madame St. Estèphe, and the disapproving sniffs of Marie, who could not refrain from murmuring to her husband: "What a waste. She will not appreciate such things . . ."

These ostentatious presents were not quite Sophie's style, but still they were magnificent. Certainly, it was very generous of Raoul, and she felt almost guilty, for she would never have thought him capable of buying her so many treasures.

Marie kept stroking the gown with envious fingers. "It really is not your colour, Sophie," she added spitefully.

"Nonsense, nonsense," Raoul interrupted. "I like bright gowns. A bit more rouge on Sophie's cheeks and she'll look as smart as any girl from Paris. What did you say, uncle?"

He turned to François St. Estèphe, who had remarked something about, "That must have cost you a pretty penny."

Raoul grinned. "Not a bit of it. After all, I can't afford to have Sophie's illustrious patron thinking I'm snubbing her with worthless gewgaws simply because she hasn't a possession of her own except what he gives her. Mustn't be seen to be close-fisted. I always say if you put out you get double in return."

The men obviously thought Sophie too engrossed with her presents to be listening to their mercenary interchance, so Monsieur St. Estèphe expostulated: "Come now, my boy, you can't make me believe these fripperies cost you nothing."

"I can. And it's no falsehood. Remember the Italian campaign? You know how these perquisites fall into a soldier's hands, particularly if he is an officer. Fact is, the second basket proved the most expensive."

And, despite her inexperience, Sophie was not too unworldly to understand that Raoul's display of bounty was composed of possessions looted from Italian houses and palaces that the army had requisitioned, or, as he would say: they were the spoils of war that fall to the victor – just as she was! She knew she would never have any pleasures from this purloined booty.

The second basket was egg-shaped, and now Sophie's fingers delved unwillingly among the contents. Here were embroidered kid gloves, some creamy laces, satin ribbons, several bottles of Eau de Ninon, and a variety of pots of complexion cream from Martin of Paris, as used by the Empress Josephine herself . . . and Raoul's sister. All these, she knew, must have been purchased with hard cash.

"Well, little Sophie," Raoul towered above her, "I trust the trifles are to your liking."

"Yes, indeed, General," she said quietly. "You are most kind, and I thank you for your generosity."

"Is that all I get by way of thanks?" Raoul demanded. "What about a kiss?" He bent so that his face was level with hers, and she could smell the wine on his breath. Blushing mightily, Sophie turned away her head, and felt his hot moist lips against her cheek.

Everyone laughed.

"Such modesty," chortled Raoul's father, "is a trifle old-fashioned, my dear."

But, to tell the truth, Sophie had not been acting out of propriety but revulsion. She was saved from further jocular remarks and Raoul's embrace by the arrival of the first guests, but before he went to greet them, her fiancé murmured: "I shall expect a more ardent response later, my dear little Sophie . . ."

Soon, the salons were thronged with a brilliant assembly. Officially the ball could not open until the arrival of the Emperor, so the orchestra had to be content with playing tinkling snatches of Mozart, but few of the guests bothered to listen.

The St. Estèphes kept anxious eyes on the main doors in anticipation of their guest of honour, and Raoul's mamma gave whispered instructions that the choicest platters be held back lest they were gobbled up before *he* made *his* appearance.

Sophie's head spun from the noise and proximity of so many people. Her cheeks were reddened by the women's rouged kisses, and her fingers positively ached from the men's hearty handshakes of congratulation. All eyes took turns in watching the dainty silver and white figure as she moved among the guests, exchanging polite, meaningless phrases.

For there was no one present who did not know who her family had been, and the part the St. Estèphes had played in their destruction.

To escape these knowing glances, Sophie slipped out on to the terrace. The air was cool against her burning face, and smelt sweetly of those flowers that exude perfume by night. It was a perfect evening. All trace of yesterday's storm was spent, and the deep lilac heavens were pierced with little winking stars, more beautiful than the women's jewels.

In there, she thought, gazing out towards the dark outlines of the wood, he lies sleeping. This knowledge brought her a sense of well-being. She thought of the morrow with eagerness, knowing it meant seeing the

Englishman again. Sophie could not help marvelling how the prospect of another day actually brought her pleasure, for since coming to stay at the Château d'Argent she had willed the great clock that controls all time to stop, for only that way could she avoid this hateful marriage. Yet, here she was almost wishing away the hours until dawn.

The sounds of hastening footsteps made her turn. Men were approaching. They stopped beyond the terrace's curve, and so could not see Sophie. She recognised the unmistakable voices of Raoul and his uncle. They were talking in low urgent tones, clearly confident that their exchanges could not be overheard.

"Word has just arrived that the Emperor and Empress cannot attend the ball. He sends his apologies." And François St. Estèphe added, "I believe this must have something to do with his fresh scheme for the army, whatever that may be."

Raoul swore. "How the fine folk in there will snigger behind their hands because the illustrious guests in honour of whom all these preparations were made failed to arrive."

"Who cares?" Clearly François St. Estèphe did not. "Now, at least, I don't have to waste an evening dancing attendance on the Emperor and listening to idle chatter. It gives me the opportunity to put my plan into operation."

"Not the English spy again?"

Sophie's heart lurched painfully, and she pressed one small fist to her lips.

François St. Estèphe ignored his nephew's derisive accent. "Yes, the English spy *again*. Tonight I shall lead a little hunting party into the forest that lies between this estate and the marshlands."

"Why search there?"

The blood pounding in Sophie's ears almost prevented her hearing François St. Estèphe's reply. "There is a charcoal-burners' encampment somewhere in there. Such good-for-nothings who live outside proper communities show scant respect for law, and might easily give succour to an English spy."

"I can't very well accompany you, Uncle," Raoul said regretfully.

Sophie was dimly aware of footsteps receding into the distance. Cold heaviness imprisoned her as she understood the full import of François St. Estèphe's words.

Léontine and she had not led the Englishman to safety but into a trap from which there was no escape. Some time that night fate would deliver Edmund Apsley to his worst enemy, and the warm vibrant lips that had taught her the enchantment of a kiss would soon be set in the rigor of death.

CHAPTER
SIX

THE wildest thoughts tore through Sophie's mind as she endeavoured to shape some plan to save him. She felt her head must burst with anguish. There was no one to aid her, and without her help the Englishman was as good as dead.

A sudden footfall made her turn sharply.

"Marie said you had come out here." The too-familiar voice of Raoul St. Estèphe invaded her ears, and Sophie could deduce by its slur he had imbibed a great deal of wine. In her distraught state she could not even utter a few meaningless phrases, but Raoul had not sought her out for conversation.

He stood so close Sophie could feel the heat of his body on her bare arms. "You mustn't catch cold," he whispered. "I can't permit that."

And he pulled her into his arms, locking her against his massive chest. As Sophie struggled to be free the gold embroidery on his coat grazed her chin.

"Sir," she pleaded, "release me. Someone will see us."

In answer, Raoul gave a mighty burst of laughter, and held her all the tighter. "And so? This is our betrothal celebration, is it not? What could be more natural than the two of us embracing by moonlight? I assure you, Sophie, nobody will disturb us – not even the Emperor –"

Like steel spikes his fingers pressed against her back,

and seemed to burn their way through the gown as he forced his mouth down on hers. Sophie's own hands pushed him away, but in vain.

"Your unwillingness," Raoul's voice was thick with desire, "adds a certain piquancy, mademoiselle. I am not used to ladies who do not immediately yield themselves to me."

"Please!" Her indignant cry only made him the more eager, and he buried his lips against her throat where a pulse beat in agitation.

Had the Englishman not shown her the true meaning of a kiss, Sophie might have believed all men's embraces were as distasteful as Raoul's. Memory of that other kiss made her the more desperate to escape. She sensed there was more insult than compliment in Raoul's attentions. He thought he could do with her as he would, for there was no one to defend her. His lovemaking had no gentleness or refinement. It was simply greedy and selfish gratification. He embraced in much the same way as he ate – to sate himself thoroughly.

One hand, almost as large as her entire bosom, pressed itself against her left breast. "I can feel your heart fluttering like a little thrush caught in a net," Raoul muttered, and his grasp tightened, but the Emperor's gift pricked his flesh, so that he cursed. For an instant pain loosened his hold on her and Sophie managed to free herself.

With her cheeks afire, and her eyes huge and glowing from unshed tears of mortification, she looked incredibly lovely. Tendrils of soft golden hair had come loose in the struggle, and for the man this disarray was more enticing than the former perfection.

Raoul's breath caught in his throat. "Come here," he

panted, "I've not done with you yet. We do not have to wait on any wedding ceremony. The betrothal contract is good enough for those who bother to tarry that long."

Sophie backed from him, rage clenching her jewelled hands.

"Don't you dare touch me again, sir, or I shall cause a mighty scandal with my screams, and their echo will reach the ears of the Emperor. Your guests will not be slow to relay my complaints against General St. Estèphe. Your attentions are gross and repugnant."

Even as these phrases passed her lips the seed of a plan germinated in Sophie's brain. More frantic to protect the Englishman than her own virtue, she glimpsed a tiny chance to be seized if she were sufficiently bold. Raoul's lust and her own outraged maidenhood might just provide an escape route.

"I shall not stay here to be humiliated," she stormed. "You may tell all those who ask for me how your disgraceful behaviour drove me away." Lifting the train of her ball gown with trembling fingers, Sophie turned. "Send no one after me, I pray you, general, for Vit will stand guard outside my chamber door, and attack anyone who tries to enter."

Sophie could not see Raoul's expression of utter stupefaction. He could scarcely believe his own ears! That virginal little doll had given him, Raoul St. Estèphe, for whom women were just a pleasant and easy diversion, a regular "dressing-down".

Undecided, he stood watching the small glistening figure disappear through a side entrance which led to the main staircase. If he followed her, she was clearly capable of causing a most distressing scene and hurling hysterical accusations. Yet to return to the ballroom with the explanation that his fiancée found his amorous approach distasteful would hardly enhance his military or masculine powers. To all, save the immediate family, Sophie's sudden absence must be explained away in terms of a violent attack of megrims such as overtook all the best young ladies on occasions. The guests could think what they chose, so long as they did not discover the truth. Raoul was only thankful that the Emperor had been prevented from being present. He was not to know that Sophie shared a similar relief. Under those imperial circumstances she would not have dared to flee the celebrations.

Vit rose sleepily and wagged his tail, but Sophie gave him no more than an absent-minded pat on the head. She tore off her glittering finery and tossed it on to the silk-upholstered daybed without a second glance. At the very back of the clothes press Sophie found what she needed – a brown homespun gown and cloak that the St. Estèphes would have been aghast to know she still possessed. These belonged to her fisherfolk days. Dowdy they may have been, but the cloth was warm, strong and serviceable.

She did not need to examine her reflection. Gone was the silver and white princess-like figure. In its place stood a fishergirl whose pale hair tumbled loose about her shoulders. From her new life she borrowed only soft leather riding boots, for they would be quieter and more suited to the night's work than clogs.

"You will stay here," Sophie commanded, as the dog made to follow her, "and let no one pass."

Obediently, Vit settled himself across the threshold, looking like a small grizzled lion. One eye watched Sophie hurry into the shadows leading down the back stairs.

The stableyard was dark and deserted, the only

movements coming from the animals in their stalls. In the dappled moonlight elegant carriages without horses between the shafts looked eerie and abandoned. The coachmen and footmen who had accompanied the visitors were nowhere to be seen, but muffled bursts of laughter and snatches of song suggested they were being liberally entertained in the St. Estèphes' servants quarters, confident that it would be many hours before their services were required. By then the gilded masters and mistresses would be too inebriated to notice the tipsiness of their attendants.

When Sophie entered the stable, Reinette, the sturdy little strawberry roan, pricked up her ears and whinnied softly, delighted by her visitor. Marie had made no protest when this horse was offered to her brother's fiancée, for she considered Reinette too inelegant to bear her weight.

Unlike Madame le Corde Sophie loved riding, and it mattered not a whit to her whether the mount was thoroughbred or donkey. Her equestrian lessons had not been of the orthodox sort given by riding masters to young females of good families. As a barefoot ragamuffin Sophie had learned to ride astride and bareback on pack mules and wild ponies. There was but one skill all the fisher children acquired in order not to sustain a hard tumble – to balance on the animal's back and hang on for dear life. Now she was a proper young lady Sophie found side-saddle and elegant habit more irksome than helpful.

Momentarily, she laid her face against Reinette's warm satiny neck. "You will help me get him to safety, won't you?"

The horse turned its head as if enquiring the reason for the urgency in her young mistress's tone.

"Tonight we'll need a saddle that can be used by a man," Sophie muttered, and it took her only a few moments to find an unadorned one in the tack room.

Reinette was quickly saddled, and disdaining the mounting block Sophie scrambled into the saddle. She turned the horse's head towards the arch which led into the main drive, and in her ears the sound of hooves crunching against gravel was loud enough to summon the armies from Boulogne. Yet nobody within the château appeared to hear the solitary rider trotting in the direction of the highway.

In other circumstances Sophie would have relished the idea of a ride on a warm moonlit night, but no thoughts of pleasure quickened her spirits. Every fibre was taut with the realisation that the life of the man who had placed his trust in her was at stake.

Knowing the potholes that peppered the road must impede their progress, Sophie guided Reinette on to the grassy verge which ran alongside and bordered the woodlands. Only then did she urge the horse into a gallop. Sometimes sprays of leaves caught at the cloud of hair streaming behind her, and to avoid the peril of overhanging branches Sophie had to crouch low in the saddle.

As if she understood the necessity of their mission Reinette seemed to fly across the patches of darkness and pools of milky moonlight. At such speed Sophie could hear nothing but the air whistling past and the hammering of her own heart. There was no way to tell whether she travelled in the wake of François St. Estèphe's hunting-party or if they were still somewhere behind. Now and then she reined in the horse to sit listening to the night, tensing herself in readiness for those sounds which would mean she was too late – the thunder of horses' hooves, the crack of muskets and the screams of rage and pain.

But each time Sophie paused, there was only the murmur of leaves, the sharp bark of a fox, and the sighing of the waters at the mouth of the Somme. Yet these unremarkable sounds offered little reassurance; they suggested she was already too late.

As the road curved Sophie glimpsed the moon-flecked sea in the distance, and knew it was time to turn off the road and plunge into the forest. Now, she had to dismount and lead Reinette among the trees. The wood seemed suspiciously quiet and it was difficult to hurry and tread softly. Could it be that Raoul's uncle had trapped his prey? Were Jaconnet and his friends in custody, and Edmund a prisoner – or a corpse?

At the perimeter of the camp Sophie halted. The reddish glow from the burners' fires seemed dim in the brilliant moonlight which illuminated the clearing and cast mysterious shadows among the huts and piles of kindling. Dark silhouettes passed to and fro as the men went about their work. All was as tranquil as it had been in the early morning, and indeed Jaconnet was leaning up against his hut, peacefully chewing on his stump of pipe. He looked only faintly surprised to see Sophie and Reinette, raised a hand in greeting, but asked no questions.

"I must take our friend away," she said fiercely. "Your camp is to be searched this night."

"Where will you hide him?" Jaconnet put the question that had tormented Sophie all during her ride.

She shook her head hopelessly. "Anywhere. In the forest –"

"He must have warmth and shelter or he will

die," Jaconnet said. "He is really too weak to be moved."

"If he stays here he will die." The words seemed to numb her lips as she uttered them.

"There is someone who might help you," Jaconnet chewed reflectively at the pipe stem. "Our visitor has gold aplenty in his money-belt, and the person I am thinking of would sell his own grandmother for sufficient funds to slake his unquenchable thirst for wine and idleness."

"Who is this reprobate?"

"Have you ever heard your nurse speak of one Fernand? He's a distant relative of hers who lives on the shore not far from the chapel of St. Peter the Fisher."

Sophie shook her head wonderingly. She thought she had met all Léontine's not inconsiderable family in childhood.

"I doubt she is proud of him," Jaconnet commented laconically. "He's a murderous rogue, part smuggler and part fisherman. Cantankerous too. Even his mother said that if ever he drowned in the river his body would be found *upstream*, for he always does the opposite of what folks would expect. Of course, normally he would not put himself out for anyone remotely connected with the gentry."

"Is he an old-style revolutionary?" Sophie's eyes were grey pools of despair.

"Old-style fiddlesticks! Him!" Jaconnet's laughter was reminiscent of the crows that now and then perched on the château's silver towers. "If someone told him tomorrow he could be King Fernand I, he'd have a crown on his head before you could say 'knife' – that's how ardent a republican he is! But envy ensures that he hates anyone who seems to have a better life than his. Yet your noble name will be sufficient to win his interest, unless I'm very much mistaken."

Sophie's eyes looked a mute question. Jaconnet explained: "Fernand often speaks of the time when your parents used to spend some months in each year at the château. Apparently, your papa always instructed his bailiff to turn a blind eye to the poachers, for he was aware how a starving family can make any man take what isn't rightfully his. The Comte de Fontenoy did not begrudge anybody the odd fish or rabbit for the pot, since his own estates teemed with more game than he could ever hope to use. Needless to say, Fernand took full advantage of this indulgent climate, and made a nice living by selling what he did not eat.

"By asking his assistance you may reap a harvest from a seed planted long ago." Jaconnet smiled and his teeth were very white in his blackened face. "Fernand thinks quite highly of you, little demoiselle, despite your gentle birth."

"But I have never met him," Sophie interrupted in amazement.

"When you were born your papa royally entertained not only his tenants and workers but all those living in the area. I recall it well. For even we, charcoal-burners, came in for our share of wine and choice victuals, although most folk in the outside world normally shun our grimy company. Fernand often boasts of having drunk more than at any other time in his life during your first week . . ."

Despite the desperate situation, Sophie could not refrain from laughter. "I doubt my father could have known what service he was rendering me by giving away so much wine." How curious, she mused, that seeking to help the Englishman should lead back to those old days I scarcely knew. The web of fate is composed of threads that belong to another age . . . another life.

"Fernand also recalls your mother with some gratitude. He says she had healing hands, for she once cured him of the toothache without pulling the tooth. It seems you have inherited her skill and interest in the preparation of herbal remedies. The Comtesse's still-room was so well known in this neighbourhood that folk came from far and near to ask for her advice about their own and their children's ailments. As shy as a gazelle was your mamma, but she never shunned those who needed her help."

It gave Sophie both pain and pleasure to hear these details. One day she hoped there would be time to return to Jaconnet and ask him to tell her everything he remembered about when her parents owned the Château d'Argent.

"Fernand admits to being quite sorry about the death of the de Fontenoys," Jaconnet continued, "but until the St. Estèphes took up residence here he and his cronies had a splendid time, not even bothering to hide their poaching activities beneath darkness. Then, your fiancé's family arrived and their bailiffs had orders to flog anyone who trespassed on so much as a blade of St. Estèphe grass. How Fernand hates these St. Estèphes! Calls 'em jumped-up peasants, if you'll forgive me mentioning it, mademoiselle. But, many other lowly folk share his opinion that *they* haven't the right to behave so high and mighty. I'm afraid Fernand has nothing good to say about the General." He sought a delicate way of putting something that was discussed in wine shops along the coast in the coarsest terms.

Now Sophie's laughter was ironic. "You have no need to spare my feelings, worthy Jaconnet. Nobody has bothered to conceal Raoul St. Estèphe's more wanton appetites from me, not even he. Indeed, his family regard them as an accolade, rather like some special category of medal. Let us say, they both pursue the same game, but the younger huntsman always catches her. No doubt, Fernand's loathing owes much to jealousy. But will that prove sufficient inducement to come to the help of an Englishman?"

"He is one of those who dislikes his fellow creatures, but his hatred for the St. Estèphes far outweighs his animosity for the English. It will tickle Fernand's sense of humour to hide the very man sought by members of the St. Estèphe family. And English gold will do the rest."

"I suppose this Fernand could ferry the Englishman across the Channel this very night and then *he* would be right out of harm's way?" Sophie suggested. She did not want to think of never seeing Edmund Apsley again, but if that was the price of securing his immediate safety what right had her foolish heart to delay matters?

Jaconnet shook his head despondently. "Not even if the tide be right can the Englishman make such a journey and survive. No, he must hide in Fernand's hovel until he is stronger. Fortunately, that place was among the first to be ransacked by the general's soldiers, so we do not have to fear them prying round there in a hurry. Now, I will fetch my guest so that we can depart with all speed."

Sophie put out a tiny hand to stay him, and the man gazed reverently down at the tiny pale fingers as if at some rare flower. "Dear Jaconnet, I must find the way without your help. At least I know where the chapel is. You have already done more than enough to warrant imprisonment or worse, for you and your friends. Stay here, I pray you, and remove every trace of your visitor. It might provoke too much curiosity if you were missing when Monsieur St. Estèphe's party arrives."

"But a frail woman cannot conduct a helpless man so far without help," the charcoal-burner objected.

Sophie smiled almost grimly. "Determination and desperation gives muscle and boldness to even the frailest, dear Jaconnet. Reinette will bear the Englishman's weight if you can but secure him to the saddle."

"But –"

"We have tarried too long already," she said sternly. "Fetch monsieur here, please."

Jaconnet took the small hand and shook it heartily. "Mademoiselle, you have your mother's beauty, and also the brave spirit that once made the name de Fontenoy renowned among heroes." He turned away so that she would not see his eyes glistening with an emotion they had not shown in many a year.

In Jaconnet's hands the Englishman seemed to weigh no more than a feather pillow. Sophie's heart gave an anguished lurch as she saw how pale was Edmund's face. His eyes were closed as if in sleep.

"Is he . . . ?" she started a question she could not finish.

Jaconnet shook his head. "He swooned from pain, I think, as soon as I lifted him. He will not be able to sit on the horse."

"Then you must tie him across the saddle," Sophie said, "and we must hope that the movement does not do the wound too much harm. We have no other choice."

Very gently Jaconnet laid Edmund Apsley across Reinette's unprotesting back, and secured the unmoving body with stout hempen ropes.

"It's just as well he's unconscious," commented the charcoal-burner, "for this must prove the least pleasant way to travel. These knots should hold until you reach your destination, and I've brought along the medicines you prepared." He slung a small skin pouch on to the pommel, and then put the reins into Sophie's outstretched hands.

"Go quickly, mademoiselle. At least the moon is bright enough to show you the way through the woods and across the marsh."

"How can I thank you?" Sophie asked simply.

"By keeping yourself and this gentleman safe. God be with you, child. Know well that no one here will betray you."

Reinette trod gingerly as if fearing to disturb her precious burden.

Sophie had known her task would be difficult, but she had not envisaged it would be the most arduous she ever attempted, and more than once she regretted refusing Jaconnet's assistance. It would have been hard going for a strong man, let alone a diminutive girl in long skirts.

She had not taken many steps into the forest before her forehead was beaded with perspiration and her palms so moist with tension and effort that the leather reins stuck to them, chafing the soft flesh, but Sophie was too anxious even to feel this soreness. An impossible dilemma confronted her. To travel slowly meant risking François St. Estèphe picking up their trail, but if she urged Reinette along too swiftly Edmund's inert body could slide from its precarious perch. In which case Sophie knew she would be quite unable to lift him back to the saddle. This dread compelled her to stop every few paces just to ensure the knots were holding. But, whenever moonlight caught Edmund's fine face Sophie wondered if her efforts were wasted – she might well be escorting a corpse.

Another fear gnawed away at her determination. There was no guarantee that Fernand would help. He could accept English gold and then sell his information to the St. Estèphes – cupidity getting the better of antipathy. Should he refuse outright to hide the Englishman Sophie could not begin to plan what she must do.

Gradually, the trees became more sparse. Now she was even more scared that Edmund would topple from the horse, for the ground sloped down towards the marshlands. So profound was this fear that Sophie took to walking sideways, one hand steadying Edmund's back and the other grasping the reins.

Then, Reinette stumbled over a rabbit burrow. The body jolted beneath Sophie's hand. Her heart rose into her throat and almost prevented breathing.

"Dear Heaven," she prayed aloud, "please . . . please do not let him fall."

But the charcoal-burner's ropes held firm and kept Edmund in place. Only when they reached the yielding levels of the marsh did Sophie realise that beneath her fingers on Edmund's back was the tell-tale spread of warm dampness. The sudden shock had opened the wound.

She halted Reinette, and examined Edmund's shoulder as best she could. There was no room for vain hope that she had made a mistake for blood was flowing warm and free through the bandage.

Wildly, Sophie gazed about her. Behind rose the dark woodlands. On either side stretched the flat open lands of the marsh, interlaced with water channels turned silver by the moon. More marsh lay ahead. How far away seemed the estuary and the coast!

"We could not have chosen a better spot to be observed had our enemies selected it for us," she muttered. Reinette snorted as if in agreement, and proceeded to crop the short lush turf.

Sophie strained her ears for the sound of galloping horsemen, but could hear nothing except the monotonous chorus of hundreds of frogs, who intermittently ceased their croaking as if they, too, were listening for some ominous noise.

"I must attend to that wound before we go any further," Sophie spoke her thoughts aloud, "else someone may spot the trail of fresh blood . . ."

She did not utter her most fearful thought – that the very life force might be drained from Edmund Apsley before she learned whether or not Fernand would harbour him.

Lifting up her drab skirts Sophie caught at the gleaming whiteness of the fine silk shift that had been worn beneath the betrothal gown. With impatient fingers she tore away the exquisite lace and ribbon border. That was worse than useless. The material itself was almost too fine for its intended purpose, and Sophie wished she had thought to change into a shift of more sturdy linen. Now it was too late. Briskly, she tore strips from the skirt until all that remained of the shift was the bodice hanging loosely under her homespun dress. She did not even consider the total immodesty of standing out-of-doors with her skirts kilted up anyhow, revealing to the world her white stockings and silken drawers. Circums-

tances were too grave for regular conventions to have
any application.

Some of the strips Sophie stowed carefully in the
pouch along with the medicaments that the thoughtful
Jaconnet had remembered. No doubt the wound would
need a clean dressing once they reached their final
destination. The rest of the silk, still warm from its
contact with her body, she managed to push under
Edmund's collar, and wad about his shoulder. The
necessity for haste meant she could give him no more
practical aid.

For an instant Sophie allowed her hand to rest against
his clammy forehead. True, she was endeavouring to
gauge his state of sickness, but there was no denying
that her touch was also an attempt to communicate
reassurance and the sort of affection she had never
before felt for anyone. The Englishman was not aware
of this or anything else. Those lips that had fastened so
hotly to hers in the early morning were now as cold and
bloodless as if they belonged to a marble effigy in some
deserted graveyard.

Grim determination hardened the young face as
Sophie took up the reins and once again began to trudge
towards the shore. Reinette trotted quietly over the
grass. For Sophie the situation was so fantastic and
terrifying that she could believe herself to be imprisoned in a nightmare.

That the St. Estèphes might have by now discovered
her absence scarcely added to Sophie's anxiety. She had
no concentration left to give to her return to the château
or an explanation of her movements, should one
be demanded. Her total preoccupation was with
the Englishman remaining balanced on Reinette's
saddle.

Eventually, the boggy ground firmed beneath her feet and became the rough stones of the wide track that in one direction ran back along the estuary towards the village of Le Crotoy and in the other wound along the coast, rising as it approached the cliff on which stood the chapel of St. Peter the Fisher.

Startled by the sudden sharp, sliding pebbles Reinette's hooves faltered.

A cry of anguish rose to Sophie's throat and escaped as a dry sob. This time the ropes had definitely grown slacker, for Edmund's body lurched alarmingly and threatened to unbalance. Sophie had to use all her remaining strength to push and tug him back to his former position across the saddle.

There was no way of determining if the wound still bled, or if the rough movements had further harmed him. Sophie's desperation threatened to break in a storm of tears, but she knew this surrender to emotion would be worse than useless. Chill rivulets of perspiration trickled down her face and tasted strongly salt on her lips. Her whole body ached with exhaustion. Yet, what other choice had she but to continue with her self-appointed task? The responsibility for Edmund Apsley's fate lay in her two small hands.

A breeze blew from the Channel and fanned her face. Out there, thought Sophie, lies his own land, his own people. The knowledge gave her little comfort. Once in England, she was sure, Edmund Apsley would not even recall the name of the Frenchwoman who had tended him.

Gradually the going, particularly for the little horse, became more difficult as the land climbed steeply from sea-level. Then, the squat outline of the chapel loomed. They were not far from their goal now.

Fernand had seen his visitors long before they drew level. He sat on an upturned keg, his back to the sea, looking morosely at nets which required mending if they were to trap any save a leviathan among fish. He felt as if he had either drunk too much or needed a great deal more to put him in a better mood. There was no way of laying his hands on money to purchase more liquor unless he sold fish, and that necessitated going fishing – an activity which scarcely recommended itself.

Sophie's heart sank as she saw Fernand's expression. Moonlight could not hide the red streaking his eyes. Even several paces away the stale wine on his breath was overwhelming.

"I am Sophie de Fontenoy," she announced softly, knowing she was giving a man, renowned for being without principles, the power of life and death over herself and Edmund Apsley.

"Old Léontine was your wet-nurse," he muttered, but whether or not this counted in her favour was impossible to judge. "I'd heard you'd become a great beauty," Fernand remarked. "You don't look one. Did someone drag you across the marsh by your hair? Though," and, he added this grudgingly, "you've got your ma's eyes. Well, Sophie de Fontenoy, what do you want of me? I doubt you've sought me out to invite me to your nuptials with that Raoul St. Estèphe blackguard." He spat delicately at her feet as if rinsing his mouth after mentioning the General.

Hopelessly, Sophie replied: "I've come to beg a favour."

Craftily, Fernand eyed Reinette's burden. "I've no alms to give. Anyhow I don't hold with beggars. Folk must pay for what they want."

"Oh, I shall pay generously for your help – with gold."

His cackle of laughter was malevolent. "That the English spy you've got there?"

There was no point in denying the truth. Sophie nodded.

"There's a fine reward on his head," Fernand said cheerfully.

She did not know if Edmund's money-belt contained more than that reward. "General St. Estèphe's uncle is seeking him even as we stand here." In a few words Sophie explained about Jaconnet's hut.

This seemed to stimulate Fernand's mirth as much as if he had just heard one of his favourite bawdy jokes. He swayed to and fro in an ecstasy of delight. Sophie wondered if he were a little mad.

At last, he spluttered, "So it's a little bit of petticoat who's been making a fool out of the general and his pestilential soldiers!"

"Will you hide him, please?" She wanted to add "for the sake of my parents' memory" but did not see that that would soften Fernand's obstinacy.

Fernand seemed deaf to the entreaty in her voice. He rubbed his huge, filthy hands together and chuckled, "That Raoul St. Estèphe is going to be hopping mad." Then, "For how long?"

A glorious smile transformed her face, reminding Fernand of days long gone. "Until he's stronger."

"Then what?"

"Will you ferry him to England?"

"For gold?"

She nodded.

"I'll carry him down to my hut." He started to walk towards Reinette.

"You will be very gentle, won't you?"

Fernand stopped and eyed the girl shrewdly and soberly. "You like this Englishman, don't you, Sophie de Fontenoy?"

"He's hurt and helpless." Her reply was evasive but it did not fool Fernand.

He grinned and displayed a fine absence of teeth. Here was rich reward indeed. Not only was he going to be paid gold, but also experiencing the exquisite pleasure of helping deceive Raoul St. Estèphe in more ways than one. There was one further question he had to ask before untying the Englishman. "You did not choose to wed the General then, Sophie de Fontenoy?"

She shook her head vehemently, and eyes that he recalled from another time sparked with anger. "How could I, a de Fontenoy, choose to wed one of *them?* It is the Emperor who commanded it."

"Oh, him." Fernand was unimpressed by the Corsican. If he had embarked on a military career he too could have achieved such dizzy heights – or so his wine cup informed him.

"Of course, I'm not saying I care much for the English," Fernand remarked gloomily, "but they're a whole lot better than those accursed St. Estèphes." So saying, he untied Jaconnet's knots and swung Edmund Apsley into his arms, while Sophie looped the horse's reins over a stunted thorn-bush, and removed the pouch of medicaments from the pommel.

"Careful how you go," Fernand warned across his shoulder. "The way is steep and slippery, but that keeps out unwanted callers." As if his arms did not bear the full weight of a grown man, Fernand nimbly descended the cliff, his bare toes gripping the rocky surface.

Sophie followed more slowly, and concluded that he must be sure-footed, for he must have negotiated this path without breaking his neck on many a dark and drunken night.

His abode was little more than a lean-to shack perched askew halfway down the cliff face. A casual observer might have been forgiven for imagining it was a derelict heap of driftwood. Fernand kicked open the door and immediately a miasma of spoilt fish and stale wine filtered out to overpower the fresh salt air.

"'Taint grand, Sophie de Fontenoy," he muttered defensively. "But I reckon your Englishman is lucky to get it."

He deposited Edmund on a straw palliasse draped with a coverlet of coney skins and then lit a foul-smelling rush lamp. Sophie felt faint in the fetid atmosphere, but reminded herself firmly that however insalubrious the place at least it was safe.

"I'll leave you to attend to him. You females enjoy fiddle-faddling about," he said contemptuously, and then peered at his guest's face. "You sure he doesn't need a coffin more than a bed?"

Shutting her senses against the squalor, Sophie hurried to peel away Edmund's blood-soaked bandages. How grateful she was to Jaconnet, for he had included among her remedies his own flask of brandy. Once again she used some of it to clean the wound. Then, as before, she anointed the shoulder with comfrey paste and re-dressed it with fresh strips of silk.

She was doing her utmost to re-button Edmund's shirt when his voice startled her.

"I had a bad dream of being dragged through darkness," he said weakly. "Yet I have been delivered from it by my good angel." He stared about him in consternation and tried unsuccessfully to rise. "But where am I?"

"Don't be alarmed," Sophie soothed him gently. "Here, swallow some brandy. This time I think it may do you more good than harm." Then, she described just how he came to be in Fernand's hut. "I have promised him your gold," she added anxiously. "I trust you will not object, because without it I doubt we can rely on his assistance."

The alcohol brought colour to the man's high cheekbones. His smile was wan but sincere. "For his trouble he is welcome to it all. But, you, mademoiselle, how can I ever repay you in adequate fashion? You have risked your life for me. Not only are you fair to look upon but you are as brave as any man. Come, let me salute you."

Blushing mightily, Sophie did not hesitate to draw close to him.

"Sweet lady," Edmund said softly, "I'm damnably weak. You must bring your lovely face nearer."

The scent of her hair was more intoxicating than any brandy. It enveloped him to exclude the rank smell of the shack. This time it was difficult to say whose lips were the first to begin the kiss.

Sophie moved back. Her eyes met his. The expression of baffled wonderment was mutual. This is not possible, thought Edmund, as the revelation flooded his soul like the sun rising: I have fallen in love with her. And Sophie's own reflections echoed his: dear Heaven, how can this be? I love an English spy. Now, I know what love can be . . .

Yet, before either could offer those first words of love which rose uncertainly to their lips, the door crashed open.

Etched against the star-flecked night stood François

St. Estèphe. His left hand was pressed heavily on a walking-stick, but the right held a pistol, levelled at Edmund Apsley's head. The man's dark smile had all the triumph of the victor.

It was the first time Sophie had ever heard him speak with such wild, high excitement. "We meet once again, Monsieur Apsley, but on this occasion there is no escape for you." He inclined his head towards his nephew's fiancée. "How grateful I am to you, Mademoiselle de Fontenoy. Your horse's hoofprints led me directly to my prize."

CHAPTER
SEVEN

In one moment love had been recognised.

In the next, utterly vanquished.

Frozen into immobility by this wicked twist of fate, Sophie could only stare as the gloating expression spread over François' face. I have destroyed him, was her first and only thought. She did not even consider her own destiny at the hands of the St. Estèphes now her complicity was revealed.

The Englishman's smile was bitter. I have only myself to thank for this, he thought dispassionately. I have been a fool and must pay the final price. How could I have allowed myself the incredible stupidity of placing my trust in *her*?

"You," he spoke coldly, and his eyes and words were directed towards Sophie, ignoring the presence of his most implacable foe, "must be the most treacherous of all your sex, but after all you are a Frenchwoman. You have acquitted yourself admirably. May I assure Monsieur St. Estèphe that his family is receiving a perfect jewel in Mademoiselle de Fontenoy. Indeed, she is the most convincing decoy ever encountered, able to lead an Englishman so prettily, and with such sincerity, to his doom. I presume you preferred me apprehended further away from the Château d'Argent to prove your own cunning. Yes, mademoiselle, you are a fitting bride for the young general. I cannot think of a more suitably matched couple."

Initially, she believed Edmund was trying to convince François St. Estèphe of her innocence. Then, she realised that he did credit her with the worst possible motives. She gazed down at the Englishman with incredulous eyes. How could he think her so base? And he would die under this misapprehension.

Edmund's eyelids closed. His head slipped back on the speckled fur coverlet. Loss of blood, exhaustion, defeat, but more than anything, disillusion, had robbed him of consciousness – and the will to survive.

With an exclamation of triumph, François St. Estèphe turned to where his victim lay. Yet, before he could take one step – and to Sophie's complete amazement – he had slumped to the floor. The stick and the firearm clattered noisily beside him, but he never uttered another word.

Only then did she notice Fernand. He, too, must have been standing at the doorway, close behind François St. Estèphe. Nonchalantly, he wiped clean the blade of his dagger, and whistled between his few remaining teeth. Then Sophie understood.

"You . . . you . . ." she stuttered, horrified.

"Aye," he nodded, and put the knife back in his belt, as if he'd just dispatched a rabbit for the pot. "I've killed him. What's one less St. Estèphe, tell me that? Whatever the season Fernand regards 'em as fair game. I've a few scores to settle with that family, my pretty."

"You did it for us?" she whispered between pale lips.

Fernand chortled. "You must think I'm a regular saint, Sophie de Fontenoy. Use your head. I did it for me, of course. I don't want to lose my head for helping you. Anyway, if he –" he jerked a less than respectful finger towards the corpse, "had got hold of yonder

Englishman, and carted him and you off to prison, what chance would I get of that gold you promised?"

Sophie could not deny that Fernand's approach, however ruthless, was practical.

"What of the search party that accompanied him?" she asked, trying to appear calm.

Fernand shook his head. "He came alone. No doubt, like a regular St. Estèphe, he thought he was being clever, and would bag the reward and all the glory for himself. When I saw a solitary horseman coming this way I made myself scarce just to see who he was and what he was up to. But, I'd best get rid of him before his men do come a-searching."

"How will you do that?"

"Dump him in the Channel, of course," Fernand explained, as if to a simpleton. "The sea tells no tales. It'll be a while before anybody discovers what has overtaken the General's fine uncle. By then, the Englishman should be back in his own country, and I shall have sufficient in my pocket to clear out of this place. I fancy a change of scene."

He knelt beside François St. Estèphe and began to go through the man's pockets, helping himself to money, watch, chain and rings. "Pity to let them go to waste," he remarked thriftily.

"If his horse returns riderless to the château, suspicions will be aroused," Sophie said, shocked at how easily she had become an accomplice.

"D'you think I'm a fool?" demanded Fernand. "I'll get rid of that nag easily. There are some gypsies camped near St. Valèry. I can sell it to them tomorrow, no questions asked, for a modest price."

"But –" Sophie began.

"Enough of your questions," he said shortly. "Dratted women are always making difficulties! You'd best get along home before somebody starts looking for you."

"I can't leave him like that," she cried, pointing to Edmund.

Fernand spat on the floor. "Why not? You can't do any more for him. I'll return by and by to make sure he's not dead, and give him a bite and sup if he fancies something."

"But, I must stay here to make him understand I did not lead him into any trap," Sophie insisted. "He thinks I'm in league with François St. Estèphe."

"Trust a foreigner to get it all wrong," returned Fernand contemptuously. "Probably can't understand French! There's no point hanging round hoping to make him see sense. He won't, because he's English. If you ask me they're all a bit addle-pated. Now be off with you, Sophie de Fontenoy, before you mar the good night's work we've just accomplished." He grinned slyly. "I suppose you'll be back as soon as you can give young Master Raoul the slip." That thought seemed to amuse him, for he laughed until he choked. "When you and he are wed I wager you'll always get the better of him!"

Which was scant consolation to Sophie.

Soft but persistent rain washed against her hot face as she rode reluctantly back towards the château. She was grateful that the downpour would obliterate any prints left by Reinette and François St. Estèphe's mount. Tears trickled down her cheeks and mingled with the rain. She was physically and mentally exhausted. Too much had overtaken her that night. Love, death, and above all Edmund's terrible accusation were hopelessly entangled, throwing her emotions in a turmoil.

Reinette's hooves seemed to tap out the thought that was uppermost in Sophie's mind – I must make him understand I did not betray him . . . I must make him understand I did not betray him.

The night was fading, and the sky already the colour of a grey goose feather when she reached the château. All was tranquil. In the misty damp the towers gleamed like old silver. Not a single lamp glowed at any window. The ball guests had all gone home.

Before going indoors Sophie rubbed down the little horse that had been such a trusty companion, and ensured it had sufficient oats and water.

Sophie slipped indoors through the unbolted servants' entrance. The steep, uncarpeted backstairs smelt musty and creaked at every footfall, but men and women, worn out by a long day of toil, were unlikely to rouse themselves sufficiently to investigate noises that might easily be made by the mice which infested these quarters.

Vit was sprawled outside the bedchamber. His tail thumped a welcome as he recognised her footstep. Only one person had been permitted entry. Léontine, mouth a little open, was sitting bolt upright in a hard-backed chair snoring gently, but she started immediately into wakefulness when Sophie closed the bedroom door behind her.

One glance at Mademoiselle's pale distraught face and dishevelled appearance caused Léontine to forget the scolding she had vowed to deliver. Instead, she drew her to her bosom in a warm soothing embrace as she had done when as a little child Sophie had fallen down and cut her knees. Then Léontine briskly set about drawing off the dirty crumpled clothes, clicking her tongue in disapproval at the shift which had become a chemise, and wrapping Sophie in a clean soft bed-gown. She washed the girl's face, hands and feet, and made her drink a whole glass of warm spiced wine. Only as she brushed the snarls and burrs from Sophie's hair did Léontine request an explanation of the night's events.

Alarm and admiration took turns at darting across the woman's worn face. Now and then, she threw up her hands as though to cover her ears, unable to bear the suspense of Sophie's tale. At last, she admitted frankly: "I never knew you were possessed of such courage, Mademoiselle Sophie. Fancy that scallywag Fernand helping you. Still, now he's so deeply involved he must keep faith to preserve his own neck and earn the Englishman's gold."

"But, how am I to convince Monsieur Edmond that my sole intention was to protect him?" Sophie turned a woebegone face towards her old rse.

Léontine stroked the now smooth hair. Evidently she shared Fernand's view that the English were a rather dull-witted people. "You must not worry what he thinks of you," she chided comfortably.

"How can I help it?" More eloquently than any explanation did that anguished question reveal to Léontine the extent of Sophie's feelings for the injured Englishman. Once more she took the girl in her arms, wishing that Edmund Apsley had never encountered Sophie de Fontenoy. Englishman or no Englishman, she was to marry Raoul St. Estèphe. To allow her to dream of an impossible romance must bring even more grief than this wretched marriage.

"As soon as possible I intend to return to him to explain," Sophie said firmly.

"First you will sleep." Léontine was equally resolute. "This afternoon will be time enough to decide how to settle matters with Monsieur Englishman. Meanwhile Fernand will take care of him. The sooner he leaves these shores the better will it be for everyone. And I can't see any reason why *I* shouldn't explain the situation to him," she added crossly. "I'll make him see reason. It's high time Fernand and I were reunited, although there's little love lost between us."

Smiling a little, Sophie teased: "Oh, I am sure you will tell your relative to mend his ways, and convince Monsieur Edmond of my innocence – even if you have to use violence on both of them!" But in her heart she knew that the only one who could persuade Edmund Apsley to the truth was herself.

She allowed Léontine to tuck her into the soft high bed, and promised to sleep. Despite closely-drawn bed curtains and physical fatigue Sophie was too alert mentally to rest for very long. She could not have dozed for more than an hour before peering cautiously between the curtains. Good, Léontine was gone. She had left Vit in her place, but he would tell no tales. Soft pinkish light filtered in around the brocade draperies, and through the closed casements the birds' dawn chorus was an invitation to rise.

The others will have retired too late to waken this early, reasoned Sophie as she slipped from her bed. At the best of times the St. Estèphes were not prompt risers. Even should they discover her absence she was sure they would believe she was taking Vit for his regular constitutional, something they insisted would be quite unnecessary if he were kept down in the stables.

Although Sophie dressed hastily her choice of gown was not without a certain awareness that the pale blue lawn, untrimmed save for a bunch of matching ribbons hanging from the bosom, set off her delicate colouring to perfection. She did not pause to put on a hat, despite the knowledge that Léontine would lecture her for venturing out in the sunlight without a brim to protect her fine complexion. Oh well, the sun is scarcely out yet, Sophie comforted herself, so its rays will not be strong enough to bronze or freckle.

"We must take him some dainty nourishment to tempt his appetite, for I doubt anything Fernand prepares will be very wholesome," she told Vit as they hurried down to the kitchens where only a few heavy-eyed scullions were lighting fires, and making half-hearted attempts to begin cleaning up the débris.

Just as the St. Estèphes despised Sophie, so their servants admired her. Her gentle manners had soon endeared her to them, so that even the supercilious major-domo – who looked down his substantial nose at everyone – would have done any favour for her.

The difference between Sophie and young Madame le Corde had been a topic of much debate among them. "They can't abide that stuck-up creature," Léontine had informed her gleefully. "She's lucky to be alive. Each time she sends back a dish from the dining-room, with one of her finicking complaints, cook vows she'll poison her by adding a few toadstools to the mushroom fricassée she dotes on!"

And Marie was certainly fortunate to have survived until her twenty-second summer, since Sophie had never sat at a meal when she did not demand that something or other be taken back to the kitchen because it was uneatable. At first, Sophie had been amazed, for the food at the château was excellent even compared with what she had tasted at the Lamberts' house in Paris. It took her only a brief while to understand that this was just another of Marie's little ways.

Léontine did not tell Sophie how the servants had commiserated with her that the beautiful Mademoiselle de Fontenoy should be forced to wed their General. Oh, that he was a fine enough soldier, all were agreed upon, but nobody relished the day when he would became master of the Château d'Argent, for he showed no civility to anyone in the social strata below his. Their sole comfort was that the little lady would make a good mistress – that is, if *he* permitted it.

So, when she begged a few delicacies, from the many left after the feast, to give to a poor family, Sophie was presented with more than enough to meet Edmund Apsley's needs. The servants grinned knowingly at each other. Here was another example of Mademoiselle de Fontenoy's amiable nature. Of course, they understood she had to rise early to accomplish such an act, for the St. Estèphes were well known as the sort who would rather burn superfluous food than give the meanest crust to a beggar, or a retainer.

Some very choice morsels found their way into her basket: a small quail stuffed with foie gras, a few golden-baked brioches, a pat of almost white butter, the cook's lightest, tiny custard tarts, and two nectarines from the south-facing orchard slopes. Sophie was even fortunate enough to collect a pitcher of fresh milk, for this was the hour the dairymaid brought the produce across from the home farm.

At the bottom of the basket, unseen by the servants, were strips of clean linen, and a small additional supply of those pastes and tonics prepared for the Englishman's benefit.

Sophie did not think it fair to take out Reinette after so brief a rest, and instead chose to walk across the gardens, through the woods and over the marshes. That might seem an over-long walk for a delicately-nurtured young female, but Sophie had been accustomed to such exertions and more from childhood; however great the distance, fisherfolk walked and used mules and horses mostly as pack animals.

Vit's large paws made flat dark patches on the dew-silvered grass as he loped beside her. Sophie was too preoccupied preparing the explanation she would offer Edmund Apsley to pay him much attention, and therefore did not notice when the dog ceased to accompany her. It was his short, warning bark that disturbed her reverie, and startled several wood-pigeons, making them fly up into the pale blue heaven.

About ten yards behind her Vit was standing, quite still, his head turned towards the château. Then, Sophie's eyes recognised what the dog had sensed or seen.

The figure of Marie le Corde.

Since Marie was not the kind who saw pleasure or benefit in fresh air at any hour, let alone such an early one, there could only be one motive for her sortie: to find out where her future sister-in-law was heading.

Even from that distance it was clear she must have hurried, for she was wearing an untrimmed morning gown that usually would never have been taken outside her boudoir. It must have been the first robe to hand. Over her head and shoulders she had thrown a shawl. Normally, it would take her maid a good half-hour to drape this satisfactorily. That morning this attention had clearly been forgone.

Sophie's heart and mind groaned in disappointment.

There was no alternative but to wait for Marie to catch her up.

Haste had given the sallow face an unusual flush. It was mere chance that had allowed her to glimpse Sophie walking purposefully through the gardens. She had only wakened because her wretched maid had not closed the shutters tightly enough and light was beginning to edge into her bedchamber. The second she saw Sophie she was determined to find out what the baggage was up to. It would delight the St. Estèphes to show the Emperor that his high opinion of the de Fontenoy was utterly misplaced, and that the General deserved to be a Marshal without the encumbrance of such a flighty creature.

So Marie had not even tarried long enough to rouse and berate Martin, who was sleeping off a surfeit of wine in his dressing-room.

The new light was not kind to her face. It showed up the traces of stale rouge and the thin, dyed tresses, and emphasised the lines etched between nose and mouth. In contrast, the morning seemed to enhance Sophie's appearance. This unspoilt beauty could only add to Marie's mistrust. Why would the girl go to the trouble of making herself presentable at such an unearthly hour unless she was contemplating a clandestine rendezvous? Taking a dog for a walk was scarcely sufficient pretext!

Marie could not come directly to where Sophie stood, for Vit barred the way, his eyes malevolent, and his jaw hanging open to exhibit cruel teeth. Clearly, he knew how Marie felt about him and reciprocated the dislike.

"Call that brute away from me," Marie's voice intruded harshly on the early calm.

"Vit!" Sophie said softly. "Come here to me. There's a good fellow."

The dog ambled over to Sophie and crouched at her feet.

Clutching her shawl, Marie approached gingerly. "Where do you think you're going alone at this hour? It is most improper. Do you imagine my brother would approve of your scandalous behaviour?"

"I am not alone," Sophie reminded her. "Vit is here."

Marie scowled. "But where are you going?" she persisted, and, without waiting for the answer, continued, "I suppose it is some secret tryst with a lover. How long do you think Raoul will tolerate your coldness towards him? I saw how you smiled at all the gentlemen last night – *all*, that is, except my brother who has been inveigled into marrying you, a penniless nobody. As for your shameful treatment of him, and that fine display of outraged virtue which made him a laughing-stock before so many important people, that didn't convince me of your much vaunted purity! Quite the opposite, in fact. Imagine the fiancée retiring from her own betrothal ball! It's unheard-of. I can tell you, few believed that tale of a sudden headache."

She paused for breath, her eyes raking Sophie's flushed cheeks for some confirmation of these accusations. So long as nobody approached the truth, Sophie did not care what they believed.

"You are quite mistaken, madame," she returned coolly, "I have no lover, secret or otherwise. As to shameful treatment, your brother's conduct scarcely became a gentleman or one who sets such store on what influential people think of him. As to marrying me, he has only to tell the Emperor he has no wish to proceed with the ceremony –"

Marie elected to ignore the suggestion with all its difficult implications. "Where else could you be going but to meet some fellow? And what have you hidden in that basket?"

Here was the question Sophie feared, but before she could answer another voice interrupted, "Oh, Mademoiselle Sophie," it said reproachfully, "you are a naughty girl. I told you to forget such foolish fancies."

To judge by Léontine's perspiring face and heaving bosom, the woman must have run all the way to where the two young women were standing.

"Ah." Marie's smile was triumphant. "So what has the virtuous Mademoiselle de Fontenoy done that is even disapproved of by her doting old nurse?"

Sophie's smoky eyes were huge as Léontine seized her basket, lifted a corner of the white cloth covering its contents, and then said severely, "I knew I was right. You really should not give your own victuals to those too idle to work for their own."

"What idle folk?" demanded Marie, bemused by the sudden turn of events which did not meet with her expectations.

"Poor fisher families who live down by the estuary. I'm sure you will agree, madame, when I tell Mademoiselle Sophie that giving help only makes 'em the more idle. Yesterday evening I did note mademoiselle putting aside some of the food served to her, and suspected where it must end up. I hurried down this morning to prevent such foolishness."

Sophie had never before heard Léontine lie so glibly and stared at her in amazement. Marie took this for silent fury and was delighted that some kind of rift existed between girl and woman.

"Oh, kitchen scraps!" Madame le Corde backed

away from the basket as if it contained the plague, fastidiousness outweighing curiosity. "Don't imagine Raoul will sympathise with your bountiful instincts, Sophie. Let those who work fill their bellies. The others must starve, and serve 'em right."

Léontine nodded in lugubrious approval.

"My brother won't want you traipsing about the countryside visiting such raffish folk, especially as there's a murderous English scoundrel on the loose. Nor will he care much for you giving away the fine food we put before you." Clearly, she had forgotten the criticism she normally cast on the cook's efforts. "No wonder you're so skinny –" The way Sophie's gowns skimmed her slender form had rankled with Marie ever since the two of them had first met.

She turned imperiously to Léontine. "And you, woman, will take that basket and throw its horrid contents to the pigs while Sophie comes indoors with me."

"Of course, madame." Léontine managed a small bobbing curtsy which Marie failed to notice contained more mockery than respect. "I shall go straight to the pigsty."

The apparent alacrity with which Léontine was prepared to do Madame le Corde's bidding may have convinced the latter that her authority was being respected, but Sophie, who knew her nurse too well, did not believe she was going anywhere near the pigsty. In fact, the little push Léontine gave to propel her along with Marie made her quite sure that the basket would shortly be taken to its intended destination. After all, Madame le Corde was unlikely to examine the pig troughs to verify that her orders had been obeyed.

Raoul was just descending the staircase when Marie and Sophie re-entered the château. From his dark expression all the servants knew it wiser to keep well out of the way. His mood owed much to the amount of drink he had consumed the night before to drown his chagrin at the virginal little doll's blistering rejection of his lovemaking. The rest of the evening he had felt everyone was privy to his discomfiture, and the smiling countenances were really laughing at him.

Delighted to catch her brother in such ill-humour, Marie immediately regaled him with an account of Sophie's misdemeanour, an account so embellished that it sounded as if the girl had purloined cartloads of foodstuffs to distribute to ne'er-do-wells far and wide. Having delivered her piece Madame le Corde tripped contentedly up to her own chamber.

Sophie made to remove herself from the glowering, silent presence of her future husband.

"And where do you think you're going, mademoiselle?" he demanded.

"Nowhere in particular," came her small response.

Holding open the door of the salon, Raoul said sternly: "Kindly step in here, mademoiselle. What I wish to say is hardly meant for the whole household's ears."

Sophie had no choice but to enter the salon, still littered with unwashed glasses and plates.

"Now listen to me," Raoul raised his voice so that the ears of the household would have to be very deaf indeed not to hear his tirade. "I shall not tolerate your unnatural behaviour. Had Marie not espied you heaven knows where you'd have gone gallivanting."

"I did not imagine I was doing anything that the occupants of the château would disapprove of," Sophie said carefully. She kept her lustrous eyes lowered lest rebellion alert Raoul to the great secret.

The General's scowl deepened and gave his features a heavy, brutish look. It was quite true he did not entertain the slightest affection for Mademoiselle de Fontenoy, but that she should not for ever be fawning on him, hanging on his every word, hoping to catch a smile or an endearment, yearning for his kisses, like any other female he had ever come across, was as much an insult and a challenge as a man slapping his cheek with a glove.

Yet, he could scarcely call out the Emperor's Jewel to settle this score once and for all. He did not want to love but to dominate her. The only way to be her master, he was convinced, was to break her spirit entirely, and then she would not have the impudence to think or act in any way other than that dictated by himself and the other St. Estèphes.

He attempted to grasp her wrist, but Vit's deep-throated growl made him reconsider. Raoul's hand dropped impotently to his side, and he directed his fury at the dog.

"When we are wed, mademoiselle, that animal will be banished to the stableyard where it belongs. You will have a yapping little lapdog as befits a lady of fashion. No normal female would choose to have such a monstrously ugly brute as a pet. Ladies prefer those whining scraps of fur and gristle that need as much warmth and cosseting as themselves. Then you can carry it in your muff, tie ribbons around its neck, and let it share your chair the way other women do."

"I don't like to see animals made into toys," Sophie objected.

"I promise that you will when we are married." His grim tone had more threat than promise in it.

Marie le Corde, who had made it her business to pass

the half-open door of the salon, was content to hear her brother's voice charged with anger. Her fear was that somehow Sophie, whom everyone admired so much, would manage to twist Raoul around her finger until he knelt at her feet in adoration. If no man was prepared to do this for her, Marie was certainly going to do her utmost to prevent it happening to Sophie.

She could not comprehend what people saw in that chit. Even Martin, who should have known better, had the audacity to say on one occasion: "Mademoiselle Sophie is a true beauty with a nature any man might desire in a wife, so that I do not see her lack of dowry as a disadvantage. Especially as she has merited the Emperor's favour –"

This was an opinion he did not express again before his wife, for she had flown into a tantrum and declared he was being disloyal to the St. Estèphes who had done so much for him!

"In future, Sophie de Fontenoy," Raoul addressed his fiancée as if she were one of his subordinates, "you are forbidden to step beyond the gates of the château without my permission and a suitable escort. Do I make myself clear?"

Seeing how downcast Sophie's face became he smiled victoriously. The best way to handle this filly was to keep her on a very tight rein.

Sophie realised she was virtually the St. Estèphes' prisoner. Her heart grew sombre. Now, she would never see Edmund Apsley again, never be able to explain how she had only sought to ensure his safety, and never again feel his lips against hers.

CHAPTER
EIGHT

SOPHIE sat forlornly by the open window of her boudoir. Her eyes gazed over the grounds, shimmering in the heat haze, but her heart roamed far beyond. Never would she have a caged song-bird as a pet, for she was in a position to understand just how such a creature must feel. This brief respite from General St. Estèphe's exultant attitude was her sole consolation. Now that he had exercised his power to command, Raoul seemed to believe he could treat his bride-to-be as if she were no more than a jointed doll which could be made to do its owner's will.

Her mood alternated between anger and misery, which resulted in a tight band of tension about her temples. She tried to sew, but thoughts of Edmund Apsley made it impossible to concentrate on neatly embroidering the initials "St. E" on the fine linen dinner napkins intended as part of her trousseau. Yet, what use was there in dwelling on someone she would never meet again? All it did was to make her despair the more of her future.

When Léontine bustled in, her face red and shiny as befitted someone who had not long since trudged across the marshes in the noon-high sun, Sophie jumped up, heedless of the sewing that slipped to the floor, "Did you see—?"

She was not allowed to finish her urgent question.

Pressing a finger warningly to her lips, Léontine said carefully, "I think it is time you took Vit out for a walk, despite the heat, don't you, mademoiselle?"

Pausing only to tie the violet ribbons of a deep-brimmed straw-plait bonnet beneath Sophie's chin, they sauntered down to the gardens. The heavy warmth kept everyone else indoors. If Raoul were watching from some shadowy embrasure he would only have seen his fiancée, in a white muslin afternoon gown sprigged with violets, leading her dog, accompanied by her maid. Even he would not suspect any secrets were being discussed.

Once they were where their voices were drowned by the soft but insistent plish-plash of water from the small dam which fed the lake, Léontine gripped Sophie's fingers. "We daren't talk indoors, my lamb. There may be eavesdroppers behind every door. Down in the servants' hall no one can talk of anything but the General forbidding you to step beyond the gates. All agree he is a bully and would lock you in if he found you disobeying him."

Sophie waved an impatient hand as if dismissing any reference to Raoul. She did not doubt him capable of going to any lengths to secure his own ends.

"You guessed I have not been to the pigsty," Léontine said slyly.

"Naturally. Did you talk with him?" Sophie asked.

Purposely, Léontine misunderstood her. She nodded, "If anything, that Fernand has grown more cantankerous and evil than when we last met."

"Yes, yes. But the Englishman, what did he say?"

"Nothing."

Sophie's eyes darkened with apprehension. "Why?"

"Because he was sound asleep," came the laconic

reply. "He should get plenty of rest for that wound to heal. I left the basket with Fernand, who scoffed at the food, saying such morsels were fit only for babes-in-arms, not grown men in need of strength. I told him to feed them to his guest all the same, for I doubt Fernand's fish stew can be swallowed by any but the very strong. He was cooking it when I arrived, and I've never seen such a nasty –"

Sophie knew that if she allowed it Léontine would not only expound on the dubious ingredients in Fernand's pot but also on how such a dish should be properly prepared. "It is no longer a simple matter of making him listen to me," she interrupted. "Now I cannot visit him –"

Léontine shrugged. "So what? I shall carry all the nourishment and medicine Monsieur requires until he is sufficiently strong to make that boat crossing. As for your explanation, I'll give it him, which ought to be good enough even for an Englishman. There is no longer any necessity for you to go to Fernand's."

Sophie divined that while Léontine smarted with fury at how the General had confined her, she was secretly relieved that Sophie could have nothing more to do with Edmund Apsley. My one true ally, the girl thought grimly, is against me in this, even though her motives are of the best.

The afternoon tranquillity was suddenly disturbed by a party of horsemen rattling across the bridge into the courtyard. The sun flashed on spurs and harness. Sophie de Fontenoy knew fear. Had these men come with fresh news of the English spy's whereabouts?

"Quickly," she said to Léontine. "Let's go closer so that we can hear what has happened."

Raoul, his father and brother-in-law came out on to

the steps to greet the visitors, who were members of François St. Estèphe's search party.

"We have come to report that so far not a trace of that accursed spy has been found," their spokesman announced.

The General and his father seemed surprised rather than dismayed.

"My uncle has not yet returned," Raoul explained. "We assumed he would be with you."

"Oh no. Monsieur St. Estèphe went off alone sometime last night without saying why or where he was heading. We imagined that afterwards he would come back to the château, which is why we are here with our report."

"Typical of my brother François," chuckled old Monsieur St. Estèphe, rubbing his hands. "That is a good sign. It means he has picked up the spy's scent and is following it. He's a regular bloodhound and won't give up until the Englishman is in his power. I wager that before long he'll send word that his task has been successfully completed." Almost pityingly he surveyed the travel-stained and weary horsemen, and added, "Single-handed as becomes a true St. Estèphe."

During this interchange the only people to experience tremors of alarm were those two who knew the truth, Sophie and Léontine. They glanced covertly at each other without speaking, but both were thinking, how long could it be before François St. Estèphe's absence was pronounced suspicious and a full-scale search party sent out to find him?

Then Raoul caught sight of Sophie standing behind the newcomers. He called harshly, "Pray, what do you think you're doing here, mademoiselle? It is not fitting for you to flaunt yourself before strangers. Go indoors at once and sit with my mamma and sister as befits a respectable female."

The horsemen had not noticed Sophie previously, but now they turned astonished eyes on the delicate girl whose cheeks were scarlet with mortification. All felt embarrassed at witnessing a young lady being treated in such a peremptory manner. Martin le Corde's expression betrayed his sympathy as Sophie passed quickly by with head held high, Vit and Léontine trotting in her wake.

Indoors, the tears of rage and humiliation she had tried to restrain started to fall, and she fled upstairs to avoid Madame le Corde's malicious satisfaction.

It was with reluctance that Sophie came down again just before dinner. Her head was elegantly proud, with the gleaming hair swathed to resemble a coronet, but inside she felt a sinking sensation rather than any appetite. As she had sponged away the tear-stains and changed her gown in readiness for evening, Sophie had reasoned with herself: if I do not go down he will send his sister or mamma to fetch me. That would be a further humiliation. I shall show them that a Fontenoy is not to the cowed by such as they.

The clamour of raised voices coming from the small silk-hung parlour startled her. Most unusually, they did not belong for once to Raoul and Marie. Apparently, Monsieur and Madame St. Estèphe felt the need to take their son to task. To judge by the surly growls punctuating any pauses, he was receiving it with rare good grace.

Sophie had no compunction about listening in on this curious conversation which so much affected herself.

"You cannot continue to treat the girl like some raw

recruit who needs licking into shape," expostulated his papa.

"No indeed not," his fond mamma chimed in. "Mark my words, Raoul, it might reach the Emperor's ears. She may even get word to him herself. Would that not be rather foolish? He may not expect you to dote on his jewel, but he does believe you will accord her the usual delicacy found between affianced couples. Come now, my dear boy, you will not gamble your glittering future away by a pigheaded refusal to treat the little de Fontenoy with greater kindness –"

"And you know how much I want a grandson," Monsieur St. Estèphe grumbled gloomily. "You'll never get a child if you're enemies before the vows are taken. Come, Raoul, could you not act in a more lover-like fashion?"

"Oh, do, dear boy, try to appear more fond," Madame St. Estèphe pleaded. "Why not. take her out riding by the estuary, since she enjoys such pastimes?"

Sophie overheard her fiancé snap something about riding with such a silly little creature hardly being his idea of good sport. "In fact, it's a downright waste of an afternoon!"

"We know well enough you would rather idle your time away in some low tavern," retorted his mother pettishly, "with a wench on either knee . . . and we also know how such things end up."

Here Monsieur St. Estèphe's wheezy chuckle could be heard. Sophie thought it contained a hint of envy. "Come now, Clothilde, there's nothing wrong with that. Shows our Raoul's a real man. But, in this case, my son, you would not be wasting an afternoon, rather investing it in a good cause."

"All right. All right," the General returned without any enthusiasm. "But do cease your nagging."

"You will remember to ask her nicely," urged his mother. "Don't just order her to accompany you."

Sophie managed to slip into the drawing-room just before the parlour door opened. An enigmatic smile pursed her lips as she waited to receive the General's reluctant invitation.

It was after dinner that Raoul chose to speak to her. Rather ostentatiously the others had made excuses to leave the couple sitting at table, although Marie was reluctant to retire and Martin had almost to drag her from the dining-room.

Raoul helped himself to another glass of claret. It must be confessed he had already imbibed a good deal more than usual. He considered Sophie with a somewhat gloomy expression.

"My dear," he began, and the endearment sounded as if it issued from between gritted teeth, "tomorrow we are going . . ." He paused, cleared his throat, and tried again, "How would you fancy a ride beside the estuary tomorrow?"

If Raoul had known what a tremor this question had caused in Sophie's breast his vanity would have been flattered, but then he would not have understood her reason.

All through the dinner she had scarcely eaten, Sophie was toying with one idea. If the only way she could go outside the château gates was in Raoul's company, somehow this chance must be fashioned to suit her purpose – which was to visit Edmund. The problem was how to go with the General and lose him on the way.

She propped her chin on clasped fingers and regarded him with great, solemn eyes. "After your disgraceful behaviour during the betrothal ball I really feel the less time you and I spend together alone the better," she said in a small voice.

Raoul swallowed hard, and his already florid cheeks took on a deeper hue. If she did not agree to come out with him, he thought irritably, then his parents would for ever be at him to find some other way of showing his devotion to this creature. "I do understand it must be tedious for you cooped up in the château and the gardens," he said, and then very truculently added, "It's not much fun for a fellow either to spend his brief furlough forever in the company of his parents and sister. Come, say it would be a pleasant change to be away from here for just a few hours."

"A brief ride would be acceptable, I suppose," Sophie said reluctantly. "No doubt you would prefer to spend your valuable free time in a congenial wine-shop."

The General's eyes glittered with a hard angry light, for he expected Sophie to deliver a homily on how he should mend his ways, so that he was somewhat caught off balance by her next words.

"Of course, you could visit a wine-shop," she began tentatively, "whilst I . . ."

Sophie was prepared for the dark brows to draw together in heavy suspicion. "Whilst you what?"

Her tone was melodious and conciliatory. "I know you have little time for religion, General, so it would give you no pleasure to go to the chapel of St. Peter the Fisher on the shore. You recollect it? Where fishermen go to pray for a safe voyage and a good catch, and fisher brides make offerings before their weddings in order that the union be fruitful, and later take their babes for good health and fortune. I, too, was carried there as a

baby, according to the local traditions. I should so like
_"

"Superstition!" growled the prosaic-minded General, yet his brain was already responding to the lure of the wine-shop. "So you want to visit this chapel place?" he added with a faint sneer.

Sophie clasped her fingers the tighter and nodded. Nothing would be gained if he decided to accompany her.

"Well," Raoul drawled, as he considered a plan of campaign. If he permitted her to go to this chapel, which was apparently important to her and quite inoffensive, she would think the better of him. Meanwhile an hour or so spent in the wine-shop would be welcome. "I have decided to grant your wish, little Sophie," he smiled at his own magnanimity.

Her anxiety was so intense that Sophie could not speak.

"You and I shall leave here together, and then go our separate ways. There is no need to tell the others of our arrangement," the General added swiftly. "I'll permit you to spend exactly two hours at your fisherman's chapel, and then escort you home. Do not take advantage of my soft-heartedness by keeping me waiting."

"Oh, thank you, Raoul," she said gratefully, and smiled because they were both conspirators now.

When Léontine learned of Sophie's plan, she was alarmed, but proud of her girl's daring and obstinacy.

"You have all the valour of the de Fontenoys," the whispered. "But what if . . . ?" A host of potential hazards rose to her lips but remained unsaid, for Sophie would not listen.

"I understand the perils," she said gravely. "You can help me by obtaining some little delicacies from the kitchen for our invalid, and stowing them in Reinette's saddle-bag. I will hide fresh unguents and bandages in a pouch beneath the skirt of my riding-habit."

Sophie dressed herself with the utmost care to go out riding with her fiancé, experimenting at placing the velvet hat with its horn buckle on her golden curls at several dashing angles before finding the one which seemed most to suit. Marie insisted on being present during these preparations, and watched with jaundiced and suspicious eyes. Grudgingly, she had to admit the girl did look very well in the brown broadcloth riding-habit with its black velvet collar, and cream lace peeping out at throat and wrists.

"I'm glad to note you are taking such trouble for my brother," she sniffed. "It's more than kind of him to waste his time amusing you."

Side by side, Raoul and Sophie rode demurely along the long tree-lined drive, knowing many curious eyes must be watching until they were out of sight. Once beyond the gates, the General raised his hat in brief salutation. "I shall see you in exactly two hours outside the chapel. Don't be late. Now I must be on my way – I shall ride quicker without you. You have only to follow this road and you will soon reach your destination." As an afterthought for her safety, he added, "Don't worry too much about meeting the English spy –"

Fortunately, he was too impatient to be about his own affairs to notice how her eyes widened. "He must be well out of this district by now, since Uncle François still has not returned."

Raoul did not stay for her reply. He spurred his great horse into a gallop and soon all she could see of him was the cloud of rising dust marking his progress towards the village of Le Crotoy.

Fernand was neither surprised by Sophie's arrival nor particularly impressed that she had managed to dupe that young fool of a general, although that she had done so did give him an excuse for several cackles of malevolent laughter. He readily agreed to watch the road while she went inside.

Edmund was asleep, which gave Sophie time to tiptoe about setting out the things she had brought for his comfort. Then she stood watching him. His face had grown thinner but this in no way detracted from its handsomeness. His even breathing suggested a quiet fever-free sleep. It was as she stood gazing down on this stranger who had brought her such an unexpected mixture of heartache and joy that she noticed the brightly-hued miniature on the floor beside his couch. It had fallen from his pocket.

The likeness was of a dark, spirited beauty with laughing eyes and lips.

If the Englishman kept this image with him then the lady had to be somebody special. Hardly his mamma, to judge by the current hair-style and neckline. Therefore the unknown was his betrothed – or even his wife.

Anger scorched her cheeks. Those kisses had meant nothing more to him than relief in the midst of danger, perhaps made the more enjoyable by that danger. He had merely taken advantage of being in the company of an impressionable, unescorted female. In which case he was as bad as Raoul, and she was a simpleton to believe him to be otherwise.

Sophie was furious with herself for having been so swayed by those kisses, to have imagined they meant more than dalliance, but even more angry with the man who had introduced her to these delights.

Edmund was dreaming. He was walking through a splendid garden with a beautiful gold-haired maiden at his side. They were surrounded by wondrous scents. The aromas were so pervasive that as he awoke they still lingered in his nostrils.

Verbena and rosemary. Such a blend he associated with only one person. He opened his eyes and saw the girl from his dream. The anger at her betrayal surged back. "So you have returned," his tone was cold and contemptuous. "This time, no doubt, you have led your General here to finish off his uncle's work."

Sophie forgot the gentle reasoned explanation she had intended to present. Rage at how he had purposely deceived her made her eyes blaze, and she burst out: "How dare you of all people accuse me of perfidy? I have risked everything for your safety, Monsieur Edmond, yet you insist on believing I am base."

Edmund stared at her, amazed by her righteous anger. How beautiful she was with that heightened colour. He longed to believe her, yet his training told him it was wiser to doubt. Never before had any of his secret missions clashed with an emotional interest, and he recalled how when he first became an agent for the government a very senior personage had advised, "Now then, young Apsley, I offer you this counsel. Bear it in mind, however experienced you become in our strange twilight business: never let your personal feelings blind you to reason, especially in the case of some young filly with a neatly-turned ankle."

Edmund had never forgotten. He was no longer "young Apsley", and, seasoned by his many adventures, it was now he who offered callow youths advice. At the time of his life when he should have known better it seemed he had fallen into a trap composed of his own tumultuous feelings, feelings he had never before understood, baited with a lady whose loveliness was as undeniable as the stars in heaven but in whose total integrity it was safer not to trust.

Sophie's torrent of detailed explanation ended with one breathless question: "What makes you believe I am as devious as the serpent in the Garden of Eden?"

"Because you are French,' he retorted.

Sophie threw up her hands in exasperation. "You cannot understand or believe me because *you* are English and it is a known fact that they are all numbskulls!"

Yet, even while she uttered these words, her heart kept insisting it loved this impossible man who, it seemed, belonged to another.

Sophie sighed. "We are wasting valuable time," she said finally. "Come, let me see your shoulder."

Edmund was silent while she cleaned and anointed the wound and re-covered it with fresh linen. He watched the small frown of concentration which creased her brow gradually ease itself away. "Ah, it is healing beautifully," she murmured her delight.

He could not contain his next remark. "Only thanks to you, Mademoiselle Sophie. Truly, I have never encountered a woman like you in my life."

Her lips took on a sarcastic curve. "Not even your wife, monsieur?" she returned sweetly.

"I have no wife." He was obviously puzzled at her mistake.

A blush invaded Sophie's throat. "I suppose the dark beauty whose likeness you carry with you is, then, your betrothed?"

Edmund grinned. The perfect angel was fallible after all. She was jealous. This awareness gave him a jolt of pleasure. He held out his hand for the miniature and

smiled down at the familiar face. If he survived to tell
this tale, how *she* would chuckle!

"Serena is my one and only sister. A dear person,
although she has a somewhat fiery and rebellious tem-
perament." As he spoke, Edmund watched a variety of
emotions flit across Sophie's face. He recognised she
was struggling with embarrassment, and to give her
time to compose herself he went on to explain about
Serena's children, and the part she and the man who
was now her husband, Ralph Sherwood, had played in
bringing about the downfall of François St. Estèphe, or
Mr. Francis Stevens as he had called himself in England.

"So you are not promised to anyone, Monsieur
Edmond?"

He shook his head. "There is no girl who sits and
waits and weeps for me." Then, very grimly, "Unlike
you, Mademoiselle Sophie, I have made no vows to
marry."

Her eyes became matching grey clouds. For a short
while, she had forgotten her own imminent marriage,
but the Englishman's words had plunged her back to
reality. There was no real cause to rejoice because *he*
was free. She certainly wasn't.

"Ah, if only I could be released from this vile
arrangement."

He could not ignore the desperation in her voice.

"Tell me, Mademoiselle Sophie, if you could be
freed from your bondage," he asked carefully, "would
you take the opportunity to escape?"

"How can you ask?" Sophie laughed mischievously,
and he noticed the dimple in her chin make its charming appearance. "Are you perhaps thinking of sending
an English gunboat to snatch me away?"

He smiled a little sadly. "Believe me, I would if I could, but I fear that by the time such arrangements could be made your fate would already be sealed."

Sophie shook her head impatiently. "We are chasing moonbeams with our words. Don't let us talk of the impossible. Tell me instead, do you like books, music, wine and flowers? Do you dance? Do you –"

He began to laugh, and lay back weakly.

A little nettled at his reaction, Sophie asked, "What do you find so amusing?"

"Because you sound as if you are collecting information on some rare species of bird or beast, and will note all its habits down in your journal, and perhaps illustrate it with a neat pen and wash drawing. Is that not what all well-brought-up young ladies do when they are visiting strange places? How will you title me? Strange numbskull Englishman?"

It was her turn to laugh, and he thought again how marvellous the sound was. She wagged an admonitory finger at him. "Monsieur Edmond, you are being obtuse and entirely misunderstand my motives. I was but trying to make my memories of you more substantial. There is little enough time. However, now I have found a way of persuading General St. Estèphe to let me go outside the château grounds I can return to you. Then you will tell me your favourite novel, the dish you enjoy most, and the name of your horse."

"No." The word was stern and final.

Sophie believed he was teasing. "What, Englishman, do you fear to give these trivial details to a *dangerous* Frenchwoman? Then, indeed I shall have to remember you as 'strange numbskull Englishman'!"

"You must not come back here for any reason whatsoever." Edmund Apsley's tone allowed no argument.

The brief happiness that had lit Sophie's face faded to leave it sad and troubled. "Do you never want to see me again, Monsieur Edmond?" This was no valiant attempt at coquetry, as the break in her voice betrayed.

Slowly, he shook his head.

"Then, I'll manage it somehow. I swear I shall not be seen coming here," Sophie persisted.

"I intend to be far away very soon – certainly before you have found a suitable pretext to assuage the General's suspicions," Edmund said. Half of him believed it might be better if matters could be so arranged.

"I did not realise you were so obstinate."

"Why should you?" he returned. "We have spent no more than a few hours in each other's company, and know nothing of our mutual characters."

"That may be true," Sophie murmured. "But, at first, your manner was more cordial."

"A young lady should not allow herself to be swayed by first impressions," he advised. "Let this be a lesson."

"Now, you sound like one of those foppish young jackanapes my cousins Lambert kept introducing me to in Paris," expostulated Sophie.

"Do you truly believe I never wish to see you again?" Edmund's voice was quiet.

"What else am I to think?"

He took hold of her wrist and gently but firmly pulled her close to him. She did not attempt to resist and as their lips met her arms stole around his neck in the most natural way. They kissed with a passionate desperation, wanting to prove something that so far remained unspoken.

Unwillingly, Edmund released her. "Dearest Sophie," he murmured, "that must convince you of how much I want to see you again, but I cannot allow you to run any more risks for me." His smile was weary. "I shall never forget you or what you have done for me."

Reluctantly, Sophie looked at the face of the half-hunter watch pinned to her lapel. How unfair was the passage of time – two hours had travelled at the speed of one. As if to emphasise this, Fernand unceremoniously pushed upon the door.

"That scurvy wretch who calls himself a general is on his way to the chapel. He's riding slowly. Probably drunk a skinful! Hope he falls off and breaks his neck." The old reprobate grinned, cheered by that idea. "But we can't rely on it, so if you want to be there afore him, young Sophie de Fontenoy, you'd better get going."

She gazed at Edmund, indecision straining every feature.

Gently, he raised her hand to his lips. "This must be farewell, Sophie. Heaven bless you." Only then did he know this was the woman he would trust with his heart and his life.

Sophie could scarcely speak for fear of weeping. His last sight of her must not be tear-stained. "God keep you safe, Edmond." She turned and fled outside.

As Fernand had so aptly described, Raoul had indeed "drunk a skinful". He had also engaged in certain amorous exchanges with a girl whose name he thought might be Germaine. All this contributed to his mellow, unobservant mood. When he saw Sophie waiting dutifully outside the weather-beaten chapel door, he smiled complacently. The afternoon had run to plan. He completed failed to notice her desolate expression.

Little conversation was attempted as they trotted home. Sophie was free to wonder if Edmund's embraces had intended to convey a message similar to hers, or were they just a rake's way of passing time? Once back in England would he even recall her name?

She could not know that as soon as he was alone Edmund Apsley began to devise a fantastic project, which his good sense urged him to forget. Whenever he closed his eyes he saw Sophie de Fontenoy's flower-like face. Her image acted as a spur to the wildest scheme imaginable, made all the more reckless because he was a man alone on enemy territory with only one good fighting arm.

CHAPTER
NINE

WHEN Léontine brought Sophie a large bowl of hot coffee and milk the following morning it was accompanied by a piece of news. Raoul St. Estèphe and Martin Le Corde had been summoned urgently to Boulogne, and might not return for a few days.

Sophie felt almost lighthearted in the knowledge that she would not have to endure Raoul's company for an entire day. So long as he was not present she could try to pretend the marriage was a long way off instead of set for the thirtieth of the following month.

"I heard the General tell his papa that he would make some enquiries along the way about his uncle. They're getting a bit worried because there's still no word from him." Seeing Sophie's eyes darken with anxiety she added comfortably, "As they are going to Boulogne they won't do much searching hereabouts for a while. By the time they do, *he* should be far away. Fernand, too, I shouldn't wonder."

Sophie placed the bowl on the floor beside her bed, for Vit always lapped up the last dregs of her morning coffee. "Dearest Léontine," she cajoled, patting the dog's huge shaggy head, "could you leave the château without anyone asking questions?"

Léontine considered the beautiful appealing face, and said crossly, "For your sake, I suppose I could manage it. Cook did mention there is a salmon to collect from a fisherman on the estuary. I'll offer to fetch it. Most of the servants come from Paris anyway and wouldn't know a mackerel from a sardine. They could be sold any old fish. Nobody will prevent me going. None of 'em – men included – relish traipsing down there in this heat, particularly when an English spy might jump out and cut their throats. What is it you want me to do?"

"It won't take you far out of your way; just ask Fernand when he plans to carry his guest across the sea."

She waited for Sophie to offer her reasons, but as the girl did not Léontine concluded she must be contemplating something her old nurse would counsel against. With a disapproving sniff to show she resented being excluded from Sophie's secrets, Léontine poured an ewerful of warm water into the washing bowl and dropped in a little bag of fresh rosemary and verbena to make it fragrant. Sophie began to wash.

Léontine, who couldn't abide silence for long, remarked, "That Madame le Corde has another of her headaches." Everyone in the household knew this meant there had been some disagreement between Marie and the much henpecked Captain.

Sophie ignored the cheerful manner in which Léontine had imparted this piece of gossip, and said thoughtfully, "When I'm dressed I'll see if I can find something to soothe away the pain for her."

Léontine made a wry face. "I'm sure one of your potions will do just that, but, in my opinion, Mademoiselle Sophie, you're being overly considerate to that viper. Given the chance, everyone below stairs would dose her with an infusion of deadly nightshade! And good riddance!"

She did not realise Sophie's motive was not based on pure altruism. If I give Marie my company and attention voluntarily, thought Sophie, she will be less likely to pay much attention to my movements this afternoon, or on the morrow. Then, depending on what Léontine learned, Sophie hoped to find an opportunity to slip out and visit Edmund just once more.

Despite her "megrims" Marie le Corde was still capable of showering insults on her wretched maid. Indeed, Sophie wondered if it were not the woman's own voice that produced the headache. Certainly, she gave one to everybody about her.

"No! No! Don't hold it like that," she shouted at the maid as Sophie entered. "Do you realise, Sophie, I've told this stupid wench a dozen times to place the mirror just so, and she is still too clumsy to get it right. I suppose there is little sense where breeding is absent."

The maid was close to tears, and cast a piteous look at Sophie who said diplomatically, "I'll hold the mirror for you, Marie, if you like. But would you not prefer that I brush your hair, for I am sure that will soothe away the pain?"

"Oh, I suppose it might do something," Marie agreed ungraciously.

"First, you must swallow a little of this," Sophie held out a glass of cloudy liquid.

Madame le Corde grimaced. "One of your nasty concoctions, I imagine. I hope you have not put any of those peasant remedies in it, like bat's blood or powdered mouse bones."

Sophie hid a smile. "No, Marie, I promise it is only a concoction of vervain, most efficacious against head pains. Come, drink it."

While Madame sipped the brew and made a face to

show she did not care for the taste, Sophie straightened her pillows and half closed the shutters to keep out the bright daylight. Then, she took a clean kerchief and sprinkled it with a lotion of bergamot and rose-water and placed this against Marie's hot temples. With gentle fingers she began to brush the woman's hair, while the maid slipped out of the room carrying an extremely nervous pug dog.

Half an hour later, Madame St. Estèphe appeared to enquire after her poor daughter's health.

Marie managed to groan, "I'm well enough, Mamma. It is all Martin's fault, as you know. He will not listen when I say we need a house, and —" She looked up at Sophie, and commanded, "Brush a little harder. I think you are right about it easing the pain, unless of course it was that strange mixture. You know, Mamma, Sophie has a most agreeable touch. Better than any of my maids."

"I am pleased, dearest. Well, at least Raoul is going to wed someone who will be of use to us, which is something."

Sophie barely listened. She was thinking of Edmund Apsley.

"Good Heavens!" exclaimed Madame St. Estèphe, turning her attention away from her daughter. "The child actually looks happy."

Marie sat up immediately and scrutinised Sophie's face with suspicious eyes.

Sophie flushed, dreading they might begin probing for an explanation.

Madame le Corde sank back on her pillows, waving a hand to show Sophie should resume brushing. Languidly, she remarked, "Oh, I expect she is falling in love with Raoul, Mamma, after yesterday's ride together. You know all women find that son of yours irresistible. Dairymaids and dowagers offer him their favours."

"I'm glad that Sophie has begun to see sense," Madame St. Estèphe confessed rather tactlessly. "For, frankly, one cat-and-dog match in this house is enough to be going on with. If Sophie and Raoul intend to fight as much as you and Martin I don't think Papa and I could stand it."

"If Martin would only do as I wish we would never argue at all. He is so pigheaded," Marie complained. To Sophie she added, "Don't go imagining Raoul will be faithful to you just because you begin adoring him. He should have been a Turk, or whoever it is that is allowed a harem of wives. I don't think my brother is likely to become a single-hearted fellow even in his dotage."

How Sophie would have liked to retort, "My dear Marie, let your brother marry ten wives if it please him. All I ask is that I am not forced to be one of them."

They took her reticence for shyness, and she mused that it was better to allow them to believe what they chose, for then Marie would not start accusing her of going off to tryst with some secret admirer.

Soon, Madame St. Estèphe took herself off to her husband's study to impart the good news that Sophie de Fontenoy was behaving in a more amenable fashion, and might prove quite a tolerable little daughter-in-law, all things considered. Eventually, Madame le Corde drifted off to sleep and Sophie, her arm aching from its exertions, was free to wander into the gardens.

Léontine found her sitting in the rotunda, a dreamy smile on her lips, Vit dozing at her feet.

"Well?" Sophie started out of her reverie. "What happened?"

"Such a beautiful fish," Léontine enthused. "You never did see the like even on the tables of great Parisian houses. Cook is going to prepare it with truffles, cream and Madeira." She smacked her lips appreciatively at the very idea. "She says it is fit to put before the Emperor himself. If only the wedding feast were tomorrow cook would serve it, for such a fish deserves to be the centre-piece of a great occasion."

"I suppose," said Sophie drily, "you are going to insist on telling me the weight, length and condition of this wondrous fish. Never mind, we have nothing else to think of, have we?"

Léontine's caustic laughter was curiously reminiscent of Fernand's. Perhaps it was a family trait.

"Did you speak with the Englishman?" Sophie asked. "Did he mention me?"

Léontine nodded. "He leaves tomorrow evening."

"What, so soon?" Relief and regret fought for supremacy in Sophie's heart.

"We all wish it could be later, for at present the tide is high while it is still twilight. If Fernand were to wait until full darkness, which would be safer, he could not bring his craft close enough inshore. In his present condition the Englishman cannot wade or swim any great distance."

The girl's face became solemn. "That makes this enterprise extremely perilous."

Léontine shrugged, and said grumpily, "The whole affair is that anyway."

Sophie was so busy thinking that there might just be time for her to visit Edmund that she did not hear the rest of Léontine's words.

"I thought you would be pleased," the woman remarked.

"About what?"

"That Monsieur Edmond wishes to say farewell to you just before he leaves. I have promised to find a way to make this possible. Old fool that I am."

"He does want to see me!" Sophie's face was as radiant as if lit by the first rays of the sun. That he had expressed this desire meant that he cared something for her, and no longer believed she was treacherous.

There was no profit in her thinking that afterwards they would never meet again. Since nobody could be promised a lifetime of happiness, Sophie determined to grasp the bittersweet minutes as they arose.

"He will be waiting for you at half-past six in the chapel of St. Peter the Fisher. You will have at most fifteen minutes for your adieux."

"Why there?"

"Monsieur Edmond and Fernand reckon it is a better place for you to meet unobserved. Anyway, it will be easier for Monsieur Edmond to descend from there to the shore while the boat is more or less concealed from the road by high rocks."

"Yet that road eventually meets with the one to Abbeville," objected Sophie, "which means it is used by detachments of troops going to the town."

"Ah, that is Fernand's cunning," Léontine explained – her former loathing of him had been replaced by grudging admiration for his shrewdness. "He knows the soldiers have already searched every building, as well as all nooks and crannies on either side of the road, including the chapel and his own 'residence', several times. Therefore they are unlikely to pay special attention to that area for the time being."

Sophie was flabbergasted that Léontine was proving such a willing ally in aiding her to see the Englishman for the last time. "I note you now call him Monsieur Edmond," she teased. "What has wrought this change in your attitude towards him?"

"He and I have had a long talk," came the cryptic and unsatisfactory response.

"Do you like him?" Sophie asked eagerly.

"How can I tell?" she said brusquely. "I know nothing of him. He is the first Englishman I have ever met."

"I, too," admitted Sophie reflectively.

"Then you ought to get to know him a little better before you form an opinion." Léontine sounded quite cross.

As she was to see him tomorrow evening Sophie firmly drove from her mind any thought of visiting Edmund before then. It would be dreadful if her own impulsiveness destroyed a plan so carefully laid.

At the suggestion of Monsieur St. Estèphe, who was as fond of his bed as his stomach, the household retired much earlier than was usual, for there were no young men to sit up drinking, or Uncle François to talk interminably about his experiences at the hands of the English. Indeed, the three ladies offered no argument, since they did look rather wan and spent.

For once, Sophie could safely follow Marie's example. It was perfectly acceptable that she too should appear fatigued and untalkative. Madame le Corde had declared the weather quite impossible and vowed that such heat must break in a violent storm. So long as any storm held off until the Englishman was safely across the water, Sophie did not mind if a tempest burst heaven asunder.

Once enveloped in the thick, warm darkness of her curtained bed, Sophie had hoped to devise a scheme for getting to and from the chapel of St. Peter the Fisher without anyone being the wiser. The planning could not all be left to Léontine. She also wanted to ponder how the Englishman had managed to influence her old nurse into such an amenable state, but weariness closed her eyes before many minutes, and soon she was deeply asleep.

A terrible commotion somewhere within the house wakened her. Vit was barking furiously. Sophie sat up against her pillows, and heard someone calling urgently: "You are needed downstairs, Mademoiselle Sophie. There is important news. Make haste."

As she pushed apart the bed-curtains, alarm struggled with drowsiness, which still held her captive. Despite all their plans, could the worst have happened? Had some military patrol inadvertently stumbled on Edmund's hiding-place? In which case, tomorrow evening would need no planning.

Once Vit perceived his mistress to be in no danger he ceased his noisy protesting and sank back into slumber. With trembling fingers Sophie threw a thin robe over her night smock. She hurried downstairs, her unbound tresses streaming about her shoulders like a golden mist. Halfway down the final flight she paused to survey the scene below.

The hall was full of gyrating shadows thrown by the flames from several candlesticks. General St. Estèphe and Captain le Corde had returned. Their eyes were ringed with fatigue, and their boots and breeches thick with dust as if they had ridden long and hard. Half-a-dozen other soldiers were grouped in the main doorway. Beside these military figures Monsieur

St. Estèphe, with nightcap askew and bewildered features, clutching a candle-holder, looked a figure of fun.

Marie and her mother, curl-papers peeping from beneath lacy nightcaps, were far from pleased at this disturbance, and seemed unwilling to allow Raoul or Martin a chance to explain the reason for it.

"And I tell you here and now, Martin," his less-than-devoted wife shrilled, "if this is your idea of a jest, no doubt dreamed up over too many bottles of wine, you can just turn round and gallop back to Boulogne. Such pranks may suit your rankers in the lowest taverns," she threw a disparaging glance towards the knot of soldiers, who were trying not to smirk at witnessing their Captain receiving so public a curtain-lecture, "but it is not fitting where ladies –"

Marie caught sight of Sophie, resenting immediately how this girl could manage to look beautiful even in disarray. "You should not appear before gentlemen with your hair anyhow," she berated, forgetting the curious state of her own. "It is not seemly. Where do you think you are? Back at that fishing village? Don't you understand that now you live in the Château d'Argent?"

"Very well indeed," came Sophie's soft and ambiguous response. "But I was told to make haste. What is amiss? Have you caught the spy, General?"

Wiping his forehead with the back of an enormous dirty hand, Raoul gazed up at his fiancée and grinned. She was a rather fetching morsel of womanhood in her night attire, he was pleased to note. "Not yet, Sophie." Then, he turned to his father, and said heavily, "I regret to be the bearer of bad news, sir, but Uncle François has been found –"

"Dead!" shrieked Madame St. Estèphe. "Oh, my poor heart."

Solicitously, Martin le Corde drew up a chair and helped his mother-in-law to be seated. "Aye, madame," he said. "His body was washed up a league or so down the coast."

"How came my brother to drown?" Monsieur St. Estèphe asked slowly. "I recall he was a good swimmer when we were boys. Unlike me."

"He had no chance to swim," replied his son grimly. "A knife between his shoulders caused death. Afterwards the body was thrown into the sea, no doubt by someone who hoped the crime would remain undetected."

It was well for Sophie that all faces wore pale and shocked expressions so that hers betrayed no more emotion than anyone else's. Fernand had not been as clever as he had intended, nor had the sea proved itself to be their friend.

"But who committed this dastardly crime?" Monsieur St. Estèphe clutched at Raoul's arm.

"Surely, that is obvious. The English spy. The only way that devil could escape Uncle François was by killing him. These fellows," he jerked his head towards the soldiers, "are to begin combing the district this very night. Tomorrow, I shall send for reinforcements to help them. I swear by all I hold dear that Uncle François' murderer will not escape me even if the whole countryside has to be turned upside down."

Monsieur St. Estèphe rang for brandy. When it came he gave himself and the other men liberal glassfuls. Somehow the spirits seemed to help him bear his loss philosophically. "Well, well," he kept saying, more in astonishment than grief, "Poor old François. Still, it's a wonder he survived so long, given his dangerous secret work. He always insisted on going off on his own so that nobody could help him if he found himself in difficulties."

Why, oh why did the corpse have to be discovered now? thought Sophie despairingly. If it had been washed up the day after tomorrow the soldiers could search as long as they wanted and Edmund and Fernand would be well beyond their reach. Now, Edmund Apsley's hideaway might be penetrated before the evening tide. The sands of time she had believed to be on her side had run out all too swiftly.

"Did you ride all the way here tonight to tell us of this tragedy, my dear boy?" Madame St. Estèphe's question was muffled by the handkerchief she held to her eyes. She was weeping more from shock than grief. She disliked all unexpected events. She had never cared for François, who had exercised too much influence over her husband and always treated her as if she were a fool.

"No, Mamma, we but discovered this wicked business on our way here. We have returned this night in all haste chiefly because of Mademoiselle Sophie there."

Sophie's heart, already throbbing painfully, seemed to redouble its efforts to escape from her breast. Somehow they have found out my part in all this, she thought desperately, and stared at the soldiers, her eyes dilated with terror . . .

CHAPTER
TEN

MADAME ST. ESTÈPHE and her daughter looked accusingly at Sophie and then turned back to Raoul. "Her!" they chorused disbelievingly. "What has she to do with anything?"

Raoul did not answer their question directly. "You, my sweet sister," he said with heavy sarcasm, "will not have to put up with the husband you so clearly dote upon for many more hours, nor will Mamma be forced to writhe with anguish each time I put my boots on those silly little inlaid tables. The Emperor has had enough of hanging around Boulogne, while we cool our heels and the English thumb their noses at us. At long last, he has told us the plan he's been hatching.

"The armies – two from Holland and Hanover and three from here – are to march to the Upper Danube and teach the Austrians and Russians a lesson they won't forget in a hurry. We'll come back later and singe the whiskers off the mangy British lion. It is English gold that has encouraged the rest of Europe to attack us so perfidiously in the back." Then he laughed raucously, "But we shall be marching through Germany before the stupid English realise we have broken camp at Boulogne."

All the men, including Monsieur St. Estèphe, joined in the gale of merriment.

So immersed was Sophie in her own fearful thoughts

that she did not hear Monsieur St. Estèphe's question, but it must have been about the departure date, for Raoul replied,

"The day after tomorrow for us. The Emperor himself will quit Boulogne on the second of September."

Sophie descended the last few steps to stand before the General, her heart still beating so wildly she feared he must hear it. "So you must have come to say farewell until this campaign is over," she murmured, keeping her eyes downcast lest he detect the relief flooding them.

Madame St. Estèphe clasped her hands together as if in supplication, and gave a low wail of real misery. "Of course. The wedding will have to be postponed until your return. Oh dear, all those arrangements to cancel. My poor head aches just at the idea –"

"And Mamma," Madame le Corde interrupted fretfully, "do you realise the gowns Leroy is making for us may even be out of fashion by the time this wretched battle is won? Oh, it's too bad of you, Raoul."

"Dear ladies," Monsieur St. Estèphe's acid tone resembled that of his late brother, "could you not just this once put the glory of France before the glory of your personal appearance?"

Even Marie had the grace to blush, and her mother gave a deprecating little laugh. "We don't mean it, my dear. It's just our way, so don't scold. Anyway, this delay gives us greater opportunity to cut more of a dash. We shall have more time to turn Sophie into something fitting, too." She cast an appraising eye over her prospective daughter-in-law rather as someone does who is trying to choose a likely horse.

Sophie was too bemused by this reprieve to care what anyone said. It might be months before Raoul returned and, though she did not dare frame the thought, there was always the possibility of a soldier not returning from war.

"Then, this is going to come as something of a shock to you, Mamma." Raoul slapped his thigh, enjoying his mother's discomfiture. "For the marriage cannot be postponed."

"But –" Madame St. Estèphe quavered.

"Listen to me," her son roared. "It is the Emperor's command that we marry before I leave. At this time he is most family-minded, and has rightly pointed out that when I come home again my heir may already be waiting for me. What do you all say to that?" He gave the assembled company a triumphant grin.

Sophie's tongue seemed to cleave to the roof of her mouth. Darkness ebbed and flowed before her eyes. She thought she must faint. Certainly, it was difficult to breathe. But no one was paying much attention to the bride.

"But should we not first go into mourning for poor François?" objected Madame St. Estèphe. "We can't really have a wedding at such a time."

"We can mourn afterwards," Monsieur St. Estèphe declared emphatically. "The Emperor's will must be obeyed. But," he became anxious, "how are we to settle the arrangements in time?"

"All done, father-in-law," Martin le Corde said cheerfully. "Don't worry about a thing. We have just come from the Mayor of Abbeville who will marry the couple at eight o'clock tomorrow evening. The religious ceremony will take place at nine. Nobody could refuse us whatever time we choose, since the Emperor himself is to attend and give away the bride." He turned a smiling face on Sophie. "Well, mademoiselle, we could not keep you waiting around indefinitely to become a wife, now could we?"

"But, the wedding feast!" moaned Madame St. Estèphe. "How can we hope to feed the Emperor at such short notice? Just think, everything was so beautifully planned for the betrothal ball, and then he could not come. Now this . . ."

"I am certain that the amount of food served in this place will ensure that our Emperor has more to eat than a stale stick of bread and a morsel of mouldy cheese," countered her husband.

"Yes, yes." Madame St. Estèphe, as ever, missed the irony in these words. Then her eyes gleamed at the challenge of providing a feast fit for the Emperor at such short notice. That would make people sit up and take notice of the St. Estèphes far more than if it were the result of long planning.

Marie began to chew her knuckles in a paroxysm of agitation, and at last cried desperately, "But what are we to wear?"

Her brother surveyed her with amused contempt. "I had forgotten, my poor Marie, that you have not a stitch to cover your back, and when you step out of doors Martin has to throw his military greatcoat over you to hide your nakedness." He gave burst of derisive laughter. "Why, Marie, I do believe you have almost as many gowns as the Empress Josephine, and she is reputed to have more clothes than any woman in the world."

Marie had to content herself with casting him her most vindictive glance. For, long ago, she had learned that Raoul could get the better of her in any dispute.

"And what about the bride?" Madame St. Estèphe cried, suddenly recollecting the main attraction at any wedding. "Her gown is not yet ready."

Once again, all eyes rounded on Sophie, whose mind was a thousand leagues away from wedding finery. If the ceremony was to be at eight o'clock then there was no possibility of her bidding Edmund farewell. How could she hope to slip away unnoticed a couple of hours before her wedding?

"Well, it seems as if I shall have to wear the same gown as I wore at the betrothal ball," said Marie sweetly, "so I cannot see it will harm her to do likewise, especially as she is unaccustomed to such luxury. Hers was a very costly robe. I am sure we can find lace enough to trim a bonnet so that she has all the fitting accessories of a bride."

Perhaps she had hoped to see disappointment cloud Sophie's beauty, but the bride-to-be, so engulfed was she in despair, scarcely heard a word that was uttered. One good thing, thought Sophie wryly, I remembered to change out of my betrothal gown on that fateful night, otherwise it would not be in a very suitable condition to be worn on any occasion, let alone my own wedding.

Raoul studied the girl who was shortly to be his wife as if she were some inanimate object being offered for sale. "I want her to look her very best," he addressed this to his father. "See that she wears most of the jewels, and not merely the Emperor's gift. That will be particularly important to me. Do you understand?"

Not even Marie questioned this command.

Sophie understood full well his intention. By decking her in the jewels that had once been the pride of the de Fontenoy family he was to instil into the Emperor that this alliance had of course restored to Mademoiselle de Fontenoy her rightful property. Napoleon would scarcely have time or occasion to verify whether in fact these baubles would form a permanent part of the young Madame St. Estèphe's wardrobe.

"And what will you do for the local folk in celebration of these nuptials?" Raoul demanded.

Monsieur St. Estèphe was thoroughly taken aback. "Why, what business is it of that surly lot?"

"The Emperor is most desirous that some of the customs of the aristocrats be continued. We should appear to include the poor and humble in all that concerns our family's health and happiness." He glanced towards the slender girl around whom the whole enterprise revolved. "Besides, remember *she* is *his* jewel. It will be taken as a delicate compliment by him if he witnesses her so fêted. I would presume that she and I will return here in the Emperor's company, and he will remember the St. Estèphes of Château d'Argent with even more warmth. Remember, Napoleon will no doubt be the godfather to your first grandchild. That surely is worth a small expenditure on largesse."

"I had not thought in those terms," admitted Sophie's future father-in-law, pulling meditatively at his chin.

"We were to have fireworks," Madame St. Estèphe reminded her son. "Now that is quite impossible. There is no time to send to Paris for such arrangements. Then, we would have entertained our own guests with a sumptuous display which the villagers could have glimpsed from afar. Surely, that would have sufficed."

"I suppose I could always send a few hogsheads of cider down to the nearest hamlet," Monsieur St. Estèphe said without much enthusiasm. "Then they could toast the future of the young couple as well as the visit by the Emperor."

"But not the best cider," remonstrated his daughter.

When I was born my father gave wine to all those who lived hereabouts, reflected Sophie grimly. Now, when I am to be married, another owner of the Château d'Argent bids everyone celebrate, although only to impress the Emperor. Still I doubt that anyone like Fernand will be much affected by the promise of a few mugfuls of second-grade cider!

"The girls must go straight to bed if they are to look their best tomorrow," Madame St. Estèphe's voice rose to a squeak of panic. "No rest for me, alas. I must talk with cook about the repast. I seem to recall that the salmon which arrived this morning could provide a good enough centre-piece. I am not sure that even Napoleon gets to taste one of that size very often." Faintly satisfied by this, the lady began shouting for her servants, ringing every bell-pull she could find.

Sophie drifted back towards the stairs, and scarcely heard Raoul bid her goodnight and add with a laugh, "Tomorrow you will not retire to so lonely a couch."

The others seemed to find this a good enough joke, and their laughter followed her upstairs. As the girl wandered back to her own chamber she could hear footsteps scurrying through passages and down stairways as the indoor and outdoor servants hurried to attend upon their mistress's frantic bidding, for not only was a feast to be prepared but the entire place to be cleaned, fresh draperies hung, and a positive garden of flowers to be cut and arranged.

Léontine was waiting at Sophie's bedside. From an obscure corner of the stairs she had heard and seen everything without being observed, and had no need to ask why her little lady was shivering as if it were midwinter instead of one of the hottest nights of summer.

She fetched warm milk laced with a little Calvados and forced it between Sophie's chattering teeth. Then she chafed the icy little hands and feet in an effort to restore some life into them.

"There, there, my precious child. It will be all right. See if it won't." Léontine kept whispering this litany that had once comforted Sophie in the throes of some childhood grief.

"Oh, Léontine, you know it won't. Nothing can be all right ever again," Sophie said tragically. These were the selfsame words she had used as a little girl when refusing such comfort, and then they brought a grin to her nurse's lips. Now, they could not.

For Sophie there was no longer a way of pretending this dreadful marriage might not take place. How could she live from minute to minute, registering each sixty seconds, knowing that at eight o'clock the following evening she must irrevocably belong to Raoul St. Estèphe?

Trying to control her trembling limbs, Sophie whispered, "We must get word to him. Please, Léontine, please. I would not have him believe any trivial reason prevented me from saying farewell. In my own heart I had vowed that only death would stop me from going to the chapel." She closed her burning eyes, and added, "But I would welcome death rather than this marriage."

Léontine took Sophie's face between her two calloused hands and gave her a tender smile, which conveyed something of how she must have looked when she was a girl, before her own hopes and dreams had shattered. "Do not eat your heart out, my little love. I shall go this very dawn to explain everything to Monsieur Edmond. He will understand. Now, try to sleep."

Sophie would never have slept had it not been for the powerful effect of the Calvados. She lay awake for a few moments only, numb with her unhappiness and at the same time acutely aware of the sounds outside in the night, as if all her senses had been sharpened by grief. Did the Englishman sleep and dream of home, she wondered dully, or did he lie awake and think of her?

The wedding-day dawned cool and sweet-scented, with a gossamer mist veiling the sky. Gradually, this faded to reveal the pale blue morning that would turn into a scorching noon.

Sophie slept late, for the household was so taken up in preparation that no one bothered to find out how the bride was feeling. She awoke, heavy with lassitude. For once, the beautiful grey eyes had shadows beneath them. As she was rising, an unfamiliar maidservant appeared with coffee.

The girl explained that Léontine had been out early badgering the local fishermen for crayfish, since she and the cook had decided their tails would provide a dainty and succulent trimming to the salmon. Sophie's lips parted in a small tired smile, and the maid concluded that this was one of Mademoiselle's favourite delicacies. But, Sophie understood that whether or not Léontine returned with the crayfish, somehow her expedition must take her near Fernand's dwelling.

The maid was quite concerned at Mademoiselle's pale and tense face. Here, indeed, was a typical example of pre-wedding nerves. Gently, she urged Sophie to lie against the pillows, drink the coffee and eat a crumb or two of the freshly baked croissant.

Sophie would swallow no food, but leaned back and sipped the hot, slightly bitter brew, and listened while the maid chattered excitedly about the goings-on downstairs, delighted for a little respite from all the fetching and carrying she had been doing since before first light.

"Madame le Corde has thrown a proper tantrum and no mistake." She imparted this piece of delicious gossip, giggling. "Sent the Captain from her room, hurling her hairbrush after him. Now, her maid has the task of arranging all those wigs so that Madame may decide which one will become her best this evening. I do declare, you'd think she was the bride. Her maid said that Captain le Corde had muttered something about if she hadn't done so many foolish things to her own hair it would not be in so parlous a state."

She took up Sophie's hairbrush, and began to brush the shining tresses. "Perhaps it would not irk Madame so much, but her brother's wife will always eclipse her no matter what she puts on her face or body. Mademoiselle, I swear your hair grows more beautiful every day."

Sophie nodded listlessly, and the maid was faintly surprised that Mademoiselle did not even ask for a hand mirror to examine her own face, for surely on this day of all days even the most beautiful girl would be anxious to look her best – yet here was a bride who seemed totally uninterested in everything.

The inconsequential chatter was stilled by the appearance of Madame St. Estèphe, who shooed the maid from the room. She sank into a small cane-backed chair and fanned herself violently. Raoul's Mamma was clearly in her element. However much she pretended to be distressed by the instantaneous change in plans, it really provided her with an opportunity to exercise her energies.

"Oh dear, oh dear," she moaned. "I am utterly

exhausted. My poor head aches." This last may have been true, for every strand of hair was tightly attached to a curl paper, atop of which arrangement the large mob cap looked something like one of the balloons designed by the Montgolfier brothers. She stared at Sophie critically. "Yes, my dear, you do wise to sleep late this morning," and added with an insinuating smile, "for I am sure my son's bride will need all her strength."

In truth, Madame St. Estèphe had expected a maidenly blush to paint Sophie's cheeks, or at least that the huge eyes would be modestly lowered, but there was no reaction whatsoever, and she began to wonder if the Fontenoy creature's extreme virtue (which her son had much bemoaned as being utterly out of fashion and unfair to a soldier who has little time to spend on courting) was really the result of total ignorance of life.

Hurriedly, she began to explain the duties of wife to husband, but Sophie held up her hand to staunch this effusive and unappetising lecture. "Madame," she said formally, "I have walked through many farmyards, and know about such things."

Here, the woman did look shocked. She would have sworn any girl would adopt a more romantic attitude to marrying her Raoul, and said as much.

The first words of cynicism that had ever passed Sophie's lips were spoken now: "Come, madame, I do not imagine the General is approaching this union with the starry-eyed rapture of a bridegroom quickened by love, do you? He is merely obeying the Emperor's orders, like a good soldier and citizen of France."

Madame St. Estèphe's red cheeks deepened to the hue of an over-ripe plum. She would never have believed this child capable of such a statement and, lost for a suitable response, changed the subject. "My maid, who is clever at such things and keeps abreast of all that is happening in Paris, is trimming a plain straw bonnet with Valenciennes lace, similar to that of your cherusque. She thinks it will be particularly fetching if this little veil appears to be secured with nothing but fresh rosebuds, which means they must be attached at the very last moment just before your departure."

Sophie nodded, and then remembered her manners. "I am sure, madame, it will look very well if it is to your taste."

Did this girl have no opinions of her own? Madame St. Estèphe asked herself. Admittedly, she was much more malleable than dear Marie, but was that because she simply did not care about all the money and effort that was being invested in this wedding?

"The family will have a late luncheon," she considered the bride ought to know how the day was to be arranged. "Nothing too elaborate, otherwise we shall not be able to fasten our gowns." She giggled, patted her own ample stomach, and then began to count off the courses on her fingers. "Just a good soup; some hot and cold hors d'oeuvres, followed by collops of turbot and fillets of sole. There will be but one entrée, a hot quail paté which I know my Raoul adores. And, of course, two roasts – a duck and some venison, seeing it is only family. Afterwards there are to be a couple of vegetable dishes, and a few sweets, nothing elaborate, moulded creams and fruits . . . oh, and, naturally, cheese."

"But that sounds a proper banquet, madame!" Sophie could not refrain from exclaiming. "Surely no one will be able to enjoy the feast later after consuming all that."

"Don't you believe it, my child." The woman scoffed at the very idea. "The St. Estèphes are trenchermen without parallel. Since the ceremony is to be late – thank Heaven, for I can't abide those old-fashioned morning affairs, followed by a silly little breakfast – we shall all be quite famished. If you want to hear of a banquet, allow me to tell you of the feast itself. I am sure it will make your mouth water and bring colour to those pale cheeks. I defy even the kitchens at the Tuileries to produce a superior menu."

When she had finished the full recital of the feast's contents, Sophie felt slightly queasy, as if she had dined too well, for enough food and wine had been mentioned as might sustain a whole village – if not a town – for several days. Besides the different soups, and that magnificent salmon served as the remove dish, there were to be six assorted entrées, of fish, game and lamb, three poultry roasts, six entremets, and twenty-four kinds of dessert. Almost every dish had its own accompanying wine, and the champagne was going to flow as if it were pumped straight out of the Somme.

"Fortunately, that great cake, representing the victory at Lodi, was not touched at the betrothal ball," Madame St. Estèphe confided. "So we shall have it as a table decoration – only of course nobody will be told that it was not made specially for tonight."

Taking Sophie's silence for wordless admiration, the woman rattled on, "After lunch we ladies will retire to make ourselves beautiful. That will take a good few hours, will it not?" She giggled girlishly, "But the carriages must be on the road before seven o'clock if we are to arrive at the town hall on time. We cannot keep the Emperor waiting. If he is late that is another matter. The mayor will have to postpone the ceremony until his arrival."

Sophie was not thinking of the Imperial presence. By seven o'clock – if the fates were kind – the Englishman would be aboard Fernand's boat ready to put to sea on the swell of full tide. Undoubtedly, all the village's curious eyes would be directed on the wedding party's progress along the highway and therefore highly unlikely to stray seawards. This was the only particle of comfort Sophie could extract from Madame St. Estèphe's elaborate plans.

The bridegroom's mother rose, and with one hand on the door-knob, said, "That woman of yours will be here shortly with your bath water. By the way, I have instructed her to take your dog away from here before the wedding."

"No!" Sophie's cry might have melted a softer heart, but failed even to find Madame St. Estèphe's. She looked despairingly towards the vacant spot where Vit was accustomed to sun himself in the mornings. When he was not in her room she could be certain he was out with Léontine.

"My child," her future mother-in-law said, "Raoul has ordered this. The first lesson of marriage is that you cannot gainsay your husband's wishes."

Unless you are Marie le Corde, a wry voice remarked in Sophie's head.

"If that dog is still here when you return from Abbeville, I am sure Raoul will have it shot. Wouldn't you prefer Léontine to give it to some fisherman, if any can be found stupid enough to take in such a brute?"

She did not wait for any reply.

When Léontine came in, bearing an enormous copper urn of water, followed by a maid staggering beneath the weight of a second one, Sophie was standing, dry-eyed, staring into space. Vit, who had bounded in with the servants, nuzzled her hand and then retired to his usual sunny patch to snooze while his mistress was bathing. Only when the maid departed did Léontine say in her most matter-of-fact tone,

"Don't fret about old Vit, mademoiselle. You will see him whenever you choose. This evening I shall take him where he'll always be well treated."

"Then you are not coming to Abbeville to see me married?"

Léontine emptied the urns into a porcelain slipper bath decorated with cornflowers, tested the temperature with her elbow before sprinkling it with essence of roses.

She shook her head vigorously. "No, my dear child. Did I not swear to your mamma – Heaven rest her – that I would always take good care of you? Believe me, if I am party to this ceremony at town hall and church I will not have fulfilled my vow. But I am not going to talk of that now. Come. The water is just right. After the bath, I shall wash your hair. I have news for you," she paused significantly, "from our friend."

With the water lapping silkily about her shoulders, and the perfume of roses filling her nostrils, Sophie listened in bemused silence as Léontine relayed Edmund Apsley's message.

When the woman had finished there was silence apart from the birdsong outside and the tiny splashes made by Sophie's toes. "He is going to leave a letter for me behind the little Madonna in the chapel," she repeated wonderingly. "But what for?"

What difference does a letter make now, her mind demanded scornfully of her heart?

It will be something to keep for ever, returned that heart.

"I do not know his precise reasons," Léontine said carefully, "but he has convinced me of their value."

"He must be a very persuasive person then." Sophie could not recall anyone being able to convince Léontine of anything.

"He is. You are to fetch the letter this evening after his departure." The woman stared over Sophie's head as if into another place.

"How can I?" the girl's voice was quite hopeless.

"Hush, my little bird, hush." Léontine patted her cheek gently. "The wedding procession goes straight past St. Peter the Fisher, for that is the only route to Abbeville. You will not be there before seven, that is certain, but some five minutes after the hour. Obviously, to enter the chapel you must gain your fiancé's permission, but I have thought of how you may gain that. Listen carefully to me, Sophie. Everything depends on you doing just as I suggest."

Léontine spoke slowly and deliberately as if repeating a well-learned lesson, so that Sophie knew she had been schooled by the Englishman. Never before had Sophie heard such urgency and conviction in the woman's tones, and she knew that no matter what happened she must attempt to collect that letter.

CHAPTER
ELEVEN

THERE was an English expression that amused the French revolutionaries enormously since it highlighted an aristocratic failing; "as drunk as a lord". For the dispossessed it had the ring of truth. Who else but an aristo – whatever his category – could afford to become so completely intoxicated?

Raoul St. Estèphe was neither English nor a lord, but he was very drunk all the same. Much more so than usual.

"I've an excellent excuse, haven't I?" He turned belligerently on anyone who urged moderation. "I'm a bridegroom, aren't I? All bridegrooms get drunk. If a man cannot swallow some wine on his wedding-day I'd like to know when he can."

This was a question nobody attempted to answer.

The luncheon that had been planned by his Mamma was certainly a success with the family, nor did it seem particularly clouded by their recent bereavement. So busy were they eating and drinking and discussing whether the Empress might manage to accompany her husband to the evening's ceremony that they failed to notice how the bride's fork travelled back and forth to her mouth without ever the morsel of food being detached from its prongs.

"I am sure that today is more auspicious for this marriage than any other," Madame St. Estèphe said excitedly, and did not notice her son yawn behind his hand. "I have been consulting the almanac – the one that's never wrong – and do you know what it said?"

She paused dramatically, but as everyone continued eating, had to take it for granted that they wanted to hear the answer.

"The sun is now in Virgo, and this is to be a time of momentous changes in the fortunes of those born under Scorpio – like our dear Raoul . . . and also the beginning of a great happiness for those whose sign is Virgo, like Sophie."

If ever the stars are proved liars, thought Virgo's subject bitterly, surely it is now.

"Oh, Mamma, how can you believe in all that superstitious nonsense?" Marie said crushingly. "Remember, how you predicted my wedding-day would be fine? It rained solidly for twenty-four hours. You inisted that Martin's stars and mine were in total harmony." She gave a small mocking laugh and glared across at her husband, who was studying the bottom of his empty wineglass in rapt concentration as if he could read the future in it.

"And so they were, my dear, so they were," said her father comfortably. Monsieur St. Estèphe's method of dealing with unpleasant domestic facts was unfailingly to ignore them. "Of course, Raoul, by becoming a Marshal of France, is going to make us all prouder than ever of bearing the name St. Estèphe; and little Sophie cannot avoid being happily married to such as he, and giving me a score of grandchildren."

Raoul gave his bride a wolfish smile. "I am certain she shares your confidence, Papa," he declared arrogantly.

Sophie's eyes did not flinch from his. Silently, he

vowed that when they were truly man and wife he would ensure she no longer regarded him with that cold disdain which made him feel locked out of her mind and therefore less than in total command of the situation.

I must appear friendly, Sophie thought desperately, recalling Léontine's extremely logical advice. Otherwise I stand no chance of collecting Edmund Apsley's letter. The apprehension that she might be forced to pass by the chapel without stopping and entering compelled her to allow a tiny smile to play on her lips. Demurely, she dropped her eyes and appeared to be looking up at Raoul through her lashes.

Aware that this pretty display was for his benefit, Raoul gazed triumphantly about the table at his relatives. His parents were clearly relieved; his sister sourly dismissive; and his brother-in-law a little too much under the influence of Burgundy to react at all.

At last, no one – not even Monsieur St. Estèphe – could swallow another mouthful. The plates were littered with nutshells and the peel from peaches and plums. Sighing, Madame St. Estèphe rose from the table, and remarked enviously, "I suppose you men will have a little nap while we are dressing." She had eaten too well and certainly not wisely, being garbed in a loose morning robe without the constraint of a corset which normally kept her appetite as well as her figure within precise bounds.

"Of course, dear Clothilde," her husband replied thickly. "We do not require quite the same amount of time and effort to make ourselves beautiful as you do. I shall definitely take a little rest, while . . ." he looked doubtfully at his son and son-in-law.

"Rest!" snorted Raoul. "We don't want to rest, do we, Martin?"

He took his brother's-in-law silence as an affirma-
tive, although it must be said that Martin le Corde was
in no fit state to string many words together coherently.

"We have a few bottles left to kill, have we not?"
continued the indefatigable toper. "And we can play at
dice. Besides, I am hoping the soldiers will soon report
back to me with news of an arrest."

The gentlemen made only a half-hearted pretence of
rising to their feet as the ladies left the room.

"I will bring the jewel casket to your chamber when I
am dressed," Madame St. Estèphe informed Sophie as
the three of them stood at the foot of the staircase;
mother and daughter evidently not relishing the
thought of climbing upstairs after their repast. "I cannot allow a maid to carry such a precious burden."

"Don't go losing any of them," Marie could not resist
giving her envy a little freedom. "They are very valuable, and someone like you probably does not recognise
their true worth."

"On the contrary," said Sophie gravely, "I understand the full cost of this finery, Marie. How could I
not?"

But the two ladies did not really grasp what the girl
implied.

Sophie knew it would not take her long to dress, so
she determined to spend most of the remaining hours of
girlhood sitting on the floor of her room, cuddling a
rather astonished Vit. The dog was well accustomed to
Sophie's small demonstrations of affection, but quite
unused to receiving her full attention. He accepted it as
if it were his due, and his massive head turned aside
while he listened to that soft familiar voice talking of the
days when she was a barefoot child and he only a
youngster. But, of course, the dog could not know that

this was her way of saying farewell to one of her dearest companions.

She buried her face in his grizzled coat, and then looked up at Léontine, who was watching them without expression. "This new owner you have found for Vit will be kind to him?" she pleaded.

"As kind as Vit will allow him to be, I should think," Léontine retorted. "He's not going to anyone who will expect him to play the part of one of your airy-fairy lapdogs, lying on its back, kicking its paws in the air, and waiting to be tickled. Nor should I imagine the new master will sit on the floor talking nonsense to the ugly brute like you're doing."

When Léontine's tones were that gruff it meant she was hiding extreme emotion, and any show of gentleness would crumble the mask of resolve and allow the tears to flow.

"And it is not too far from here, where you are taking him?" Sophie asked yet again.

"He is not going anywhere where you will not be able to see him. Do not ask me any more now, mademoiselle. As far as you know Vit is gone and that's an end to it. Then, you will not be induced to tell the General his whereabouts, lest he take it into his head to have the animal removed from the face of the earth. He is quite spiteful enough to do that."

Sophie's arms tightened about Vit. "Oh, no, tell me no more in that case. I'll trust in your judgement which has always stood me in good stead."

Léontine looked away. "Now, we are not here to discuss the dog. Be a good girl, and let me make you ready, for I want to be away before the elegant madame comes to you with her booty."

"Then you will not see me in my full glory."

"I am sure you will look very splendid." The nurse seemed strangely offhand about attiring her for the most important day of all. "As for the jewels," she added drily, "I've seen 'em before. On your sweet mamma, and on the present lady of the house. One thing I may say about jewels, they have no loyalty and will shine as brightly around the necks and wrists of each new owner. If they didn't, I suppose folks wouldn't go about stealing 'em."

Sophie's gown looked just as magnificent on this occasion as it had on the betrothal evening, although perhaps the wearer was a fraction slimmer. Over the neatly-coiffed hair Léontine placed the charming bonnet Madame St. Estèphe's maid had concocted. The effect was quite ravishing. Holding the short veil in place were small white rosebuds faintly veined in red, as delicate indeed as the blush on a bride's cheeks, although this particular bride for once owed all the colour in her face to the rouge-pot, so pale and chill was she.

"I will say this for Madame," observed Léontine, "her maid could be a first-rate Parisian milliner. Out of a few scraps she's made you a confection that ladies would pay a couple of hundred francs to own."

She began bustling about the room, tidying up and putting away.

"Léontine," Sophie protested. "You seem in great haste to leave me. You cannot desert me now."

"Whatever put such a foolish notion into your head?" the woman said stoutly. "I wish to get Vit away from here as soon as possible. You and I will meet before long, never fear. Now, let me take a good long look at you."

She held the beautiful silver and white figure at arm's length, and pinched her own lips tightly together in order not to cry. "You will do very well, mademoiselle. Now, kiss your old nurse," she said briskly. "None of that, do you hear me, or I shall be cross." For, Sophie's eyes had begun overflowing with drops as bright as diamonds.

The girl swallowed hard, and when she looked up again the beautiful face was calm, only the eyes seeming to question why their owner had been allotted this fate.

Léontine kissed the smooth cheek, and felt the bride's cold lips against her own. "God bless you, Sophie," she said in a low voice, and with her finger traced the sign of the cross above the unlined forehead, as if she were merely bidding her good night.

"You won't forget the chapel in all the excitement," the woman reminded her.

Sophie shook her head, for she did not yet trust herself to speak.

"I swear to you, whose first months were sustained by my own milk, that it will not be long before we are together, and that I shall do all in my power to ease your future life even should it mean laying down my own." She turned away, and said harshly: "Come, Vit, you have spent enough time listening to your mistress's nonsense. We are going for a good long walk."

The dog jumped to its feet, bounded towards the door, wagging its over-long tail. Then, he looked back at Sophie and in the way his jaw opened and his great tongue lolled seemed to be smiling at her.

I must learn to bear this loneliness, Sophie thought, for soon *they* will take Léontine from me, no matter how much she vows to stay by me. Still, perhaps I may visit her as I shall Vit. "Go now," she said simply. "Bless you, Léontine, for your love."

No one – not even Marie le Corde – could deny that

Raoul St. Estèphe's bride was the most exquisite that could be found anywhere. The white and silver robe was transformed from elegant simplicity by magnificent splendour by the de Fontenoy gems. Even the Emperor's gift was eclipsed by the famous rope of pearls. Somehow Madame St. Estèphe had managed to adorn the bride with all the jewellery apart from a few rings, a pair of earrings, a brooch and a pendant which she herself wore, so that Sophie might almost be described as a perambulating treasury.

Although the bride's appearance in the hall halted the dissension raging there for a few seconds, Raoul St. Estèphe's voice was once again raised in inebriated and angry tones after he had briefly examined the girl who was soon to be his wife.

"That is sheer superstitious claptrap," he was shouting, "and something kept up by those damned aristocrats. We are the new lords and shall make our own rules. I say that she and I shall drive together to Abbeville. The rest of you can go ahead in the berline." Another glance at Sophie and he added, "Besides, she is worth a king's ransom in her present state, and needs my protection from robbers as well as that plaguey English spy. Pa is certainly no deterrent – oh, I know you were the very devil of a fighter, but not now; and Martin . . ." he grinned towards his brother-in-law who was leaning none-too-upright against the wall, ". . . is not exactly in the best of conditions, eh, old man? I shall carry a pistol in our carriage against any emergency, but I doubt anyone is going to attempt to rob the bride with General Raoul St. Estèphe at her side."

Certainly, he seemed very big and splendid and self-assured in his satin attire of crimson and oyster, although manifestly he was not as comfortable as in his uniform.

"Let us hear what dear Sophie thinks," begged his mother, whose distress was beginning to shine through her face powder. "Raoul insists it's old-fashioned nonsense for the bride and groom to avoid meeting before the ceremony and wishes to be your escort to the town hall. But I think it is so unlucky. Marie and Papa agree. Oh, do try to convince Raoul he is making a mistake."

A phantom of a grin touched Sophie's lips, and she was glad that the lace just covered her mouth. Did Raoul's Mamma truly believe that Sophie de Fontenoy had any influence over this man? Why, that was the best jest of a lifetime! She consulted her memory of Léontine's advice. Yes, matters might be steered to suit her own small plan.

"My dear madame, if you will excuse my saying so, I think you are wrong, and the General right."

Sophie was rewarded with a huge, booming laugh from her bridegroom.

"It would be much more fashionable for us to make the journey together, and safer too." She knew her next sentence to be an astute move. "Also I am convinced the Emperor would enjoy the sight of . . . Raoul . . ." Purposely, she used his first name, and saw that it had the required softening effect on its owner, ". . . and me arriving together. As to bad luck, if there is to be any, I'm afraid we have already courted it, since he and I are now only a few feet apart."

"You and I are going to shift very well as husband and wife," said the General complacently. "No cat-and-dog existence for your brother and his lady, eh, Marie?"

His sister, whose enormous green bonnet was curiously reminiscent of a coal-scuttle, and made it difficult for the wearer to look sideways, retorted, "She's amenable enough *now* because to ride with you suits her for some reason."

Sophie's heart skipped a beat. Could Madame le Corde divine her motives? But Marie's next words were reassuring:

"Unlike me, she will not arrive at Abbeville with her gown all crumpled from having to sit squeezed close to others."

Madame St. Estèphe surrendered. "I can see it's no use arguing with you two young creatures, but if anything goes awry you'll know what to blame."

She smoothed her kid gloves over her knuckles, and added, "We should leave now. It is some five minutes before seven."

Pray heaven that the Englishman has already gone abroad, Sophie's brain entreated, but common sense assured her that Fernand would not dawdle when the tide was the most important consideration. So long as the soldiers were not watching that stretch of road too keenly . . .

All the servants were standing outside, lining the bridge and the driveway, to see the wedding party move off. With a deal of heaving and puffing the St. Estèphes and the Le Cordes were eventually settled in the berline, which trundled away at a brisk pace, and was already out of sight before Raoul had handed Sophie into the small carriage which was to be driven by his batman.

Showers of rose petals were tossed in the air, and the servants' dutiful cheers echoed in Sophie's head long after they had passed through the main gates.

"Now, this is cosy," Raoul sank back on the cushions

contentedly, and took hold of Sophie's hand. "If we did not have an appointment I am sure we could find a most pleasant way of passing the time."

He was rewarded with such a charming smile that Raoul did not even pause to wonder why his bride was not demonstrating her usual coldness towards him.

"Will you please ask your man not to drive too fast?" she asked sweetly. "For I do not want my bonnet to be shaken and my gown disturbed."

"Of course, my dear one," Raoul returned amiably, and he drew closer to her so that she was almost stifled by the fumes of wine on his breath. It crossed her mind somewhat ludicrously that another man might get quite intoxicated merely from standing beside the General. "Then, I may put my arm about you," he added.

Grasping her waist with an extremely warm hand, he bawled out to the batman, "See you trot those animals or I'll have your miserable hide turned into a pair of boots for my lady here!"

He grinned at Sophie, evidently seeking her approbation for his manner of handling underlings.

"It will be pleasant to be taken care of by such a strong and forthright person," Sophie said pensively.

"I thought you must like me a little," the General built on to her sentiments, and managed to kiss her cheek through the lace veiling.

Sophie pretended to giggle, although she was feeling sick and afraid, but in the next moment Raoul had offered her a most useful cue.

"It will not be long, my girl, before you have a miniature Raoul St. Estèphe sucking at your breast who will comfort you and prevent you missing your husband while I am away at war."

"You would so much like a little boy, Raoul?"

"Of course, and so would you, like any other sensible woman."

"That is quite true." How easy it is to lie, thought Sophie, impressed by her own fluency in the art. "I know how much you hate superstition, but –"

"But what?" Now, he had the little bird in the palm of his hand Raoul could afford to be responsive.

She laughed with a coyness she did not know she possessed. "Fisherfolk, as you can imagine, prefer their firstborn to be sons."

"Even the lowly show sense at times," General St. Estèphe was prepared to concede.

"And they have an old custom to try to influence these matters."

Sophie could tell she had caught his attention, for the hand around her waist had become motionless, and the expression on his face expectant. "Something very stupid, no doubt," he said loftily, but she sensed his scorn to be false.

"I suppose it is," Sophie agreed, "but it is a very small thing that takes no time at all."

Raoul's curiosity was thoroughly whetted – perhaps because at the back of his mind there was the hope that whatever this small thing was it was somehow concerned with lechery. His question palpitated with desire; "What must we do, little Sophie, that takes no time at all?"

Despite her unworldliness, Sophie understood the drift of his mind, and smiled to herself. "It is something only the bride may do, Raoul, just before the wedding."

Slightly disappointed, he demanded, "And have you done it?"

"Since I have not been out of the grounds today there

has been no opportunity. It is too late now really, unless . . ."

"Unless what?"

Her explanation came in a breathless rush to suggest both shyness and longing. "The brides of fishermen often make a small pilgrimage to the shrine of St. Peter the Fisher, be it a church or merely some wayside chapel like the one I visited when we went out riding. There, they offer special prayers that the first child may be a strong-limbed, healthy boy."

"Oh, religion!" Raoul's heavy lip curled derisively. "You have a fondness for it, like Mamma and her silly stars."

"I knew you would not approve." Sophie's heart was pounding wildly. She felt she was playing a huge cunning fish. Would her fragile line with its tiny ephemeral bait land him? "So I shall not ask you to stop the carriage at the chapel. We are not far from it now."

She allowed her eyes to wander to the window. Eventide was falling quickly. The first stars pierced the heavens. There was a haze over the darkening sea, but no hint of storm. Somewhere out there English warships rode at anchor, vigilant against a French attack which now would not come. Not so far out, but heading in that direction, would be Fernand's little craft ploughing its way towards England. But she could detect no dark opaque shape that suggested any kind of boat. The road was beginning to climb towards the small rocky promontory on which stood the chapel of St. Peter the Fisher. One thing she had to be grateful for; there were no soldiers to be seen. Edmund and Fernand must have found their plan simple to put into operation.

Sophie glanced sideways at Raoul. He chewed his lip,

and she knew he was thinking hard. On one hand, of course he was opposed to all superstitious and religious practices. On the other, he had an almost primitive yearning to sire a son which would enhance his manly reputation almost as much as the Marshal's baton. Now that the girl from whom he had expected naught but hostility seemed to be turning out to be a co-operative little creature after all, he had no wish to thwart her. If he denied her this wish, which was so dear to his own heart, might she not become as aloof and difficult to approach as previously, which would make matters tiresome, at least in public? To yield to her in this might dispose that pretty face towards joyfulness. It must be useful to the ambitions of the St. Estèphes for the Emperor to observe how his jewel was so in harmony with the setting he had arranged for her . . .

Raoul glanced at his ornately chased fob watch, and yelled to the driver. "Stop at that scurvy little white building on the hill, d'you hear me. You know, the one that looks as if it's where the fishermen dry their nets."

"Oh, Raoul." Sophie's hands clasped together. Her gratitude was perfectly genuine.

"Now, look here, Sophie, I'll give you precisely five minutes for your prayers. See you put all you've got into them. Then, we'll have to go at a pretty lick if we are to make Abbeville in good time so don't start moaning that your bonnet is being tossed askew. If the others discover we are not behind them, the silly sheep will probably turn round and come looking for us. So be quick, and do not try my patience." He laughed uncertainly. "I suppose your virginal prayer can do our mutual cause no harm."

The manservant handed Sophie down from the carriage, for the General, overheated by wine and his somewhat restrictive finery, could only lounge against the upholstery, half-dozing as his lack of rest caught up.

Sophie climbed the shallow steps, a figure so brilliant in the evening light that she looked like some comet newly descended from heaven. There was no sound save for the sighing of the sea.

The rickety chapel door creaked as her small hands pushed it ajar. There was some solace in knowing she was to spend a few moments where *his* feet had last rested on French ground. The shadows were thick within, and held at bay only by a stump of candle someone had left burning on the altar, and a rapidly fading patch of sky from an unglazed opening high in the wall. Here, indeed, was a repository of many folks' hopes. Besides the shells, bits of coral, strips of sail and net were tiny silver votive offerings shaped like limbs and babes, speaking more eloquently than any prayer of what those who offered them sought: healing and fecundity.

The little Madonna was of blackened timber, and had been carved from an old mast. She stood on the far corner of the altar where the shadows were thickest. Sophie made straight for the statue, looking neither to left nor right. Her fingers reached behind it and contacted a paper. She drew it to her eagerly, thinking, I must read this in an attitude of prayer, and then if Raoul sends his servant for me it will appear that I am deep in my devotions.

She leaned her elbows on the altar and lowered her eyes to the paper which bore her name in graceful handwriting. Yet before she could read a word of its message a hand was thrust across her mouth. As she tried to break free and scream, the bridal bonnet slipped from her head, disturbing the pins holding up her tresses, and the hair cascaded free.

There were only two alternatives in her mind as to the assailant's identity – a footpad, or Raoul, grown suspicious, or even aware of her purpose in entering the chapel. Then she noticed the woman with a shawl about her head who detached herself from the shadows.

It was Léontine, a finger pressed to her lips.

Sophie's captor released his grip. She turned to face him, and almost swooned.

It was Edmund Apsley.

Sophie saw he was as tall as Raoul St. Estèphe, but much more finely made, without any hint of the General's corpulence. As they stood gazing at each other she was immediately aware of how diminutive was her own height.

"But you should be at sea by now," she whispered urgently. "The tide is turning, and the General waits for me just beyond this door."

"Hear me quickly, dearest Sophie. Fernand's boat is ready to cast off. Vit is on board. I came here to ask you to accompany me to England. My sister and her husband will care for you as if you were their blood relative. Meanwhile, you must know my heart is your prisoner."

Léontine grinned. "He's a clever one, this Englishman," she whispered. "The whole plan was his."

"And she only approved it once she was sure she was invited too," Edmund hissed.

Sophie's only response was to put her arms about him and kiss his lips. He held her tight, and murmured, "There'll be time for that later. We must hurry. Fernand will be growing impatient. He is keeping watch to ensure nobody spies on us from the road. In such circumstances his trigger finger will be itching, although he has been told not to shoot unless matters go ill for us."

At the very back of the chapel was a small door, so low that even Sophie had to duck her head to pass through it. There were steep, uneven steps leading down to a flat outcrop of rocks which formed a natural mole. Sometimes, when the tide was very high, the fishermen would moor their boats here to posts specially fixed for such a purpose, and climb straight to the chapel to give thanks to St. Peter for a safe return and profitable catch.

It was not easy for someone dressed like Sophie to scramble down these rocks, but Edmund guided her with his one good hand. His other arm was neatly trussed in a sling made of sailcloth, and from the confident smile on his lips anyone might believe he was completely able-bodied.

Below them, they could make out the dark shape of Vit standing alert beside the small craft. When he glimpsed Sophie he flourished his tail like a welcoming banner. However carefully they trod they could not avoid dislodging small pebbles which skittered downwards, sounding to Sophie like the thunder of cavalry, but fortunately no one on the road above seemed to hear anything untoward.

She looked back at the cliff face, and saw in the gloom the figure of Fernand stationed some half-way up. Then she caught sight of another figure on the road above. The General's batman! She squeezed Edmund's fingers to direct his attention. He nodded, but propelled her firmly towards the boat, the reassuring expression never leaving his handsome face.

The General's man stared aimlessly out to sea and then his reason for straying to the very edge of the road, and out of view of the carriage, became obvious. He drew a flask from his tunic and held it to his lips. Only while swigging a great draught of whatever it contained did his eyes fall on the three figures heading for the boat. Léontine and Edmund, in their dark garb, might have escaped his attention, but Sophie's gleaming hair and gown were too remarkable to go unnoticed. Alarm made the man toss away the flask. They heard his feet stumbling on the broken stones as he disturbed a small scree of gravel. Then he began to shout:

"General! Come quickly! General St. Estèphe!"

Matters had indeed gone ill.

Fernand did what he considered the best thing possible. He fired at the batman's legs, bringing him down with an almighty crash. To judge by the obscenities uttered, the man was far from dead, but at least he was unable to stand up or offer any assistance to his master.

Edmund thrust Sophie towards Léontine, and commanded, "Both of you get aboard. And keep your heads low, for there will be more shooting before this night is done. Fernand!" he called softly. "The tide is already on the turn. Get them away. I shall stay here and cover you. Do as I say, man."

Fernand may have been a square-built, ungainly fellow, but he could leap from rock to rock on his bare feet with the agility of a young chamois.

"No," Sophie begged over her shoulder. "We cannot go without you. Raoul has a pistol."

In answer, Edmund dug into a pocket and produced his own firearm.

Vit only had time to jump up and lick her face with an ecstatic little whine, and leave muddy pawprints over the front of Leroy's masterpiece, before he loped off to where Edmund stood in the shadow of a projecting rock. Léontine and Fernand bundled the girl aboard, deaf to her entreaties that she should be allowed to stay ashore until the Englishman was ready to depart.

As they crouched in the damp, evil-smelling bows of the boat they heard Raoul St. Estèphe begin bellowing very much like the proverbial wounded bull. He must have fallen asleep, for he sounded a little fuddled and uncertain as to just what was happening.

"You miserable cur, I suppose you were off having a crafty tipple out of my sight!" he raged at the unfortunate batman. "I'll have you flogged for this." Initially, he believed the man had somehow tripped and discharged his own pistol to wound himself. Then, he must have realised the truth.

"Sophie! Sophie! Come back here!" he screamed in a frenzy of anger. "Don't think you'll ever get away from me, and when I get you back I'll teach you a lesson you'll never forget. You ungrateful little jade! I'll sink that damned boat rather than let you set sail."

"Then you'll be the devil of a fine shot, my General, if you intend firing from up there," retorted the unabashed Fernand through cupped hands. He seemed undismayed by how reality had fallen far short of the original plan. Besides, he was savouring the discomfiture of Raoul St. Estèphe.

"I'll send the fleet after you," roared the General.

Unconcernedly, Fernand raised anchor, and began to make the sails ready.

"No, Fernand!" Sophie begged. "We cannot go without the Englishman and Vit."

Léontine held the girl tight, not merely for protection but because she knew Sophie would jump from the boat and run to Edmund Apsley's side.

"Will you be quiet, you dratted female!" Fernand

was not impressed by tears. "I've always said having women aboard is more trouble than its worth." Only Léontine understood that he was thoroughly enjoying himself in his own contrary fashion. "He won't send any ships after us. First, because he's got to get to Boulogne to give the order, and second, because they're afeared of the English fleet anchored out there," he spat contemptuously in the water. "They won't risk a drubbing from them merely on account of the General's piece o' fancy petticoat."

Raoul St. Estèphe began to blunder down the cliff.

A voice said calmly, "General, I would advise you to come no further. I am armed."

St. Estèphe paused momentarily.

"Who the devil are you?"

Edmund Apsley stepped from the shadow of the rock, and immediately the general roared, "The English spy! So it is you who seeks to carry off my bride. By heaven, I may have only injured you last time we met. On this occasion, I shall kill you for sure. You murdered my uncle."

"No, he didn't," bellowed Fernand unrepentantly, "I did."

Edmund took aim and fired, but Raoul St. Estèphe was too swift and dodged the bullet.

There was no time for Edmund to reload the pistol as St. Estèphe charged towards him. Now it was the General who took aim, holding his right arm steady with his left.

Vit, who had been standing immobile during all this turmoil, now lunged forward, growling and snapping his terrible jaws. From the howl of pain it was certain the dog's teeth had made contact with the General's flesh. The firearm clattered on to the stones. Vit was still leaping and snarling about his victim, who was hunched up, clutching his left arm as if to squeeze away the pain.

"You'll pay for what your dog has done, Sophie," he raged, "and as for the animal, I'll take pleasure in cutting its throat. As for you, Englishman –" He reached for the gun, but Edmund Apsley, with a deft flick of his foot, kicked it across the rocks.

"Edmond! Vit!" Sophie shrieked. "Run now! Fernand is about to cast off."

The dog, hearing the familiar voice, half turned. Edmund began scrambling towards the water's edge where the boat was already moving. Vit was about to follow, when Raoul retrieved the gun. He levelled it at the Englishman's back. The distance between them was too slight for him to miss.

"No," cried Sophie. "No! Not Edmond!"

Hearing her anguish, Raoul St. Estèphe smiled, but it was a very ugly smile. The passion in his bride's voice told him everything. He would ensure that she spent the rest of her days in torment for daring to care not only for an Englishman but someone other than General St. Estèphe.

The dog looked once at the boat which contained his mistress and then leaped back towards the General, his teeth seeking the man's throat. The dog's bite was certainly bad but not fatal, and the General did not relinquish his hold on the gun. He pressed the trigger. There was the customary bright flash and sharp explosion, but the bullet intended for Edmund Apsley lodged in another's head, for Vit had reared up almost as if trying to catch a ball between his teeth.

The animal lay dead at the feet of the man who would have broken Sophie de Fontenoy.

Everything had happened in so brief an instant that Edmund had sprung aboard before anyone was quite sure who had been injured. They heard Raoul's scream of pain and anger, but he was too weakened by the dog's savage attack to do more than crawl towards the water. By the time he would succeed in fetching help the fishing boat would be far out on the open sea, approaching the protection of the English fleet.

"Vit. Oh, Vit . . ." Sophie sobbed, rocking back and forth in her grief. "Oh, you big, brave creature that I loved so dearly. Why did you do it?"

Fernand muttered something about ". . . dumb animals having no more sense than women . . ." but a sharp nudge from Léontine's elbow silenced him. Then, he whispered to her, almost shamefaced at admitting any emotion: ". . . the little wench looks just like her own ma, doesn't she?" Léontine knew he was about as moved by the situation as he had ever been in his whole life.

Edmund was panting from his exertions. The wound had begun to ache, but he was curiously happy. He watched Sophie with compassion, and knew it was better to allow her to weep away her sadness. Placing his hand over hers, he murmured, "You understand that Vit sacrificed himself for us. Without him we would not be escaping to safety."

She looked up, and felt the breeze on her burning face. Above them the sails were making a pleasant flapping sound. Astern the shore of France was growing smaller, and she felt no regret at leaving. Sophie tried to smile. That Vit had given his life for them seemed to make Edmund Apsley's presence even more precious.

Léontine began to chuckle wickedly. "I was just

thinking," she gasped, "they are going to be in some difficulty explaining the absence of the bride and bridegroom to that strutting Corsican."

The thought of the St. Estèphes' complete humiliation was too much for Fernand. He laughed until the tears ran down his grimy cheeks. "Oh, I'd like to see that," he spluttered.

Using the cover of their mirth, Edmund whispered, "I suppose you are somewhat fatigued with wedding preparations —"

The tears were still rolling down her damp cheeks and her smile was tremulous, but, all the same, the little dimple appeared in her chin. "That depends."

"Any fellow who gets himself wed is a damned fool!" growled Fernand, but once again Léontine's elbow did its work.

"I realise we have known each other a very short while," Edmund ventured, "although in my mind it has begun to seem impossible that there was ever a time when I did not know and love Sophie de Fontenoy. I have little to offer, just a quiet country existence — nothing grand or fashionable. I shall no longer pursue my career as a government agent, for that is too hazardous for a married man with responsibilities. Would you share your life with an Englishman, Sophie?"

Léontine and Fernand waited almost as impatiently for her reply as Edmund Apsley.

"I would, Monsieur Edmond, but for one thing," she began.

"And what, pray, is that?" demanded Léontine. Of course, he was not good enough for her, but it was clear he would make her blissfully happy, and that was quite a lot to receive from any man, let alone one belonging to a race that gorged itself on plum pudding.

Sophie gave Léontine a reproachful little shake of the head. "I am coming to England as a refugee, completely dependent on the charity of Monsieur Edmond and his sister. I have nothing to offer as dowry."

She was not allowed to finish, for her three listeners burst into such a gale of merriment as threatened to capsize the boat.

"You appear to forget," gasped her nurse, "that you are not only wearing the Emperor's own jewel – a vulgar piece, it's true, but worth a considerable sum – but also almost all the de Fontenoy jewels."

"In fact, the Englishman will be getting himself a regular heiress," said Fernand gloomily. "These people always strike the best of any bargain." Then he brightened up, and began to cackle with wild delight. "I doubt our fine General is going to be made a Marshal after this. Not after losing the English spy, the Emperor's favourite, and all that loot, too."

"So much for your objection to my proposal," Edmund said solemnly, his merry eyes belying his tone. "Well, Mademoiselle de Fontenoy, what do you say?"

In reply, Sophie put up her lips to receive a kiss that erased all memory of her former bridegroom and the past, a kiss that opened the gates to a future paradise on earth.

AVAILABLE THIS MONTH

BLACK FOX
by Kate Buchan

In an age of reckless adventure, in a country where careless bravery is commonplace, two fiery spirits are embattled. Isabel Douglass has been betrothed to Sir Duncan Crawfurd of Glencarnie — Black Fox — by no less a personage than King James I of Scotland. A king's word can create an alliance but not love and Isabel abhors the arranged marriage with the proud Master of Glencarnie, fierce, stormy and mysterious as the mountains where his castle stands. For Isabel loves her cousin Andrew, a gentle poet, and she will not easily forsake her first love. The Black Fox finds in Isabel a determination to match his own, and battle commences . . . . .

September's other memorable Historical novel of romance, intrigue and excitement — order your copy today!

Masquerade
HISTORICAL ROMANCES

ANNOUNCING

Masquerade
OCTOBER TITLES

RUNAWAY MAID
by Ann Edgeworth

Emphatically refusing Sir Joseph Varley, the suitor of
her parents' choice, Miss Robina Westerley takes her
destiny into her own hands — and runs away. Rescue
from the worst consequences of her impulsive action
always seems to come from the lofty, imperturable
Sir Giles Gilmore — yet how can they ever mean
anything to each other, when he thinks that Robina is
only a lady's maid?

FOUNTAINS OF PARADISE
by Lee Stafford

Shipwrecked en route to Bombay, Emily Hunter finds
herself transplanted from Victorian England to an
Indian Prince's harem. Her only hope of escape from
her luxurious prison is the handsome Prince Dara
himself — and yet, when the Mutiny breaks out that
will set her free, she feels reluctant to leave her captor . . .

NOVELS OF ROMANCE INTRIGUE AND EXCITEMENT

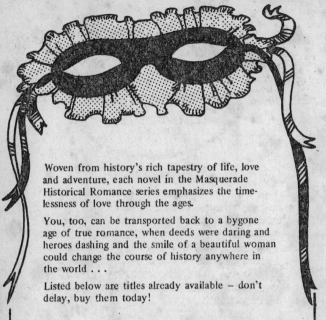

Woven from history's rich tapestry of life, love and adventure, each novel in the Masquerade Historical Romance series emphasizes the timelessness of love through the ages.

You, too, can be transported back to a bygone age of true romance, when deeds were daring and heroes dashing and the smile of a beautiful woman could change the course of history anywhere in the world . . .

Listed below are titles already available — don't delay, buy them today!

SWEET WIND OF MORNING
by Belinda Grey

Catherine did not want to marry anyone but her childhood sweetheart, Will — certainly not the dark intruder from Queen Elizabeth's court, Sir Piers Tregarron. But Sir Piers, it seemed, did not care what Catherine wanted.

HEIR PRESUMPTIVE
by Patricia Ormsby

Was Rodney Nairn the Viscount Quendon, or was he not? Five years in the Peninsular Wars had left utter confusion in their wake. He did not know if his father was dead or alive — nor whether the lady he worshipped could love him in return!

BOND-WOMAN
by Julia Herbert

Falsely accused of theft, transported to Virginia and sold on the quayside -- then Verity found that the man who owned her, body and soul, was threatening to capture her heart!

THE COUNTESS
by Valentina Luellen

When Countess Alexandreya arrived in St. Petersburg, she had already antagonised a dangerous enemy. Count Dmitri Varanov hated all women as much as she despised all men . . .